UNREAL
ALIENS

KARTHIK LAXMAN

PENGUIN BOOKS

PENGUIN BOOKS

USA | Canada | UK | Ireland | Australia
New Zealand | India | South Africa | China

Penguin Books is part of the Penguin Random House group of companies
whose addresses can be found at global.penguinrandomhouse.com

Published by Penguin Random House India Pvt. Ltd
7th Floor, Infinity Tower C, DLF Cyber City,
Gurgaon 122 002, Haryana, India

First published in Penguin Books by Penguin Random House India 2016

10 9 8 7 6 5 4 3 2 1

This is a work of fiction. None of the events described in it actually took
place—they are entirely the product of the author's imagination. The names,
persons and places portrayed in the book are either fictitious or have been used
fictitiously; they are not accurate portrayals of real persons, organizations or
places, and they should not be construed as being accurate at all.

ISBN 9780143423102

Typeset in Sabon by Manipal Digital Systems, Manipal
Printed at Replika Press Pvt. Ltd, India

www.penguinbooksindia.com

PENGUIN BOOKS
UNREAL ALIENS

Karthik Laxman is a livelihood development specialist based in New Delhi. An alumnus of BITS Pilani and IIM Ahmedabad, he has taken more U-turns in his career than Mulayam Singh Yadav and Arvind Kejriwal put together, transitioning from a software programmer to management consultant to entrepreneur to sundry other roles, before deciding to put everything aside and poke fun at politicians. He writes for *The UnReal Times* under the pseudonym, UnReal Mama.

To Mom, Dad, Priya and Anjali

Contents

Prologue

THE AGEING ALIEN emperor gazed in wonder at the sleeping form of his infant son.

It is true, he told himself for the thousandth time. The prophecy is true.

A hundred years he had ruled Mor, most of it overseeing the empire's precipitous decline. He had watched helplessly as power politics, palace intrigue and corruption destroyed institutions, disrupted governance and brought unending grief to the common people. What was once a great civilization was now a pale shadow of itself, a sick organism rotting from within, counting the days before its inevitable demise.

Softly, he whispered the words of the prophecy.

When near is the end
And shot to shit things are
A two-armed prince the gods will send
To lift his people and take them far

ix

For a long time, he hadn't believed it. Why would he? After seven sons, each greedy, corrupt, immoral and only too willing to overlook public good to further his own end, he had no reason to trust soothsayers. Consequently, when his youngest queen delivered her first and his eighth son, he had greeted the news with detached interest.

Until two of the infant's arms fell off.

One moment, the baby was a regular four-armed infant, the next, two of his lower arms separated themselves from his shoulders, and lay shrivelling in the crib. In that instant, the emperor knew. The moment that had been foretold was finally upon them.

The emperor watched with a smile as his sleeping son turned in the crib, causing the red pendant around his neck to move, sending a gentle ripple through the shimmering, near-invisible shield that protected his body.

Beside the royal cradle stood Qaal-za, commander of Mor's armies and the emperor's most trusted friend. Ferociously loyal to the realm and utterly devoted to the prince, the commander was in charge of the prince's security. Qaal-za never left the prince's side. He stood guard every minute, day after night after day, always alert, always vigilant.

The emperor turned his gaze towards the window. Outside, in the vast grounds of the castle, hundreds of thousands of Morons, the denizens of Mor, had gathered— more trickling in by the minute—as word of the prophesized prince's birth spread far and wide. Sooner rather than later, he would have to give them a glimpse of the prince.

The sudden beeping of the security monitor startled him out of his thoughts. He exchanged a glance with his commander.

Intruders, Qaal-za's eyes conveyed. Check it out, the emperor gestured. Qaal-za hesitated, eyes flitting towards the sleeping prince. Then, drawing his weapon, he stepped out of the room.

The emperor rechecked the prince's shield. This was not the first attempt on the prince's life. Thrice the enemies of Mor had sent assassins, thrice they had been neutralized by security personnel. The emperor wasn't worried. Qaal-za was a skilled warrior. Any moment now, he would return after having dealt with the intruders.

So when the emperor heard the sound of approaching footsteps, he turned around without any particular urgency. The first plasma shot punched a fist-sized hole in his abdomen. The second took a large chunk off his right thigh. With an incredulous expression on his face, the emperor collapsed to the ground, bleeding profusely.

Three assassins, wearing black and carrying plasma guns, entered the room. The leader walked up to the crib, trained his weapon on the prince's chest and fired point-blank.

From that range, a plasma shot would have decimated an adult. A child would have been shredded to fragments. The prince, however, was completely unhurt and continued to sleep with a serene smile on his face. The shield around him shimmered briefly as it absorbed the force of the shot before turning invisible again. The assassin fired two more shots and met with the same result each time.

Wounded as he was, the emperor smiled. You cannot harm him, he said, a look of triumph on his face.

The assassin nodded. He knew his weapons would not penetrate the shield. He also knew the emperor would rather die than tell them where the shield controller was. The assassin had come prepared for this eventuality. He made an inscrutable gesture, upon which his accomplice pressed a button on a panel on the wall. The chamber's retractable roof rolled open and through the widening gap descended a small space shuttle.

The emperor's eyes widened in horror as the assassin placed the prince inside the shuttle's receptacle and keyed in the launch codes. With a roar that drowned out the screams of the emperor, the shuttle soared into the sky, carrying the prophesized prince of Mor into outer space.

When Qaal-za stormed back in, he found the emperor on the floor in a pool of blood, one outstretched arm reaching for the sky.

Find him, the emperor gasped as he died in the commander's arms.

Qaal-za stared at the rapidly diminishing shuttle as it rose higher and higher, until it shrunk to a mere speck before disappearing completely.

Alien commander Qaal-za rose to his feet and, through clenched teeth, made a vow to the gods of Mor that he would travel to the furthest end of the universe if he had to, but he would find the prince and bring him back home.

In another part of the universe, a wormhole opened in the solar system midway between Mars and Jupiter, and a tiny space shuttle carrying a solitary passenger emerged through it. For a while, the shuttle drifted aimlessly. Then it adjusted its course and began speeding purposefully towards a peninsular landmass on a blue planet . . .

ONE

They Come in Peace

FROM THE MASSIVE pyramid-shaped alien mothership that drifted 100 million miles outside the Martian orbit, emerged a saucer-shaped spacecraft. The spacecraft hovered briefly, then accelerated towards Mars, rapidly gaining velocity, until it was zipping through space at one-hundredth of the speed of light.

Ten hours later, the alien spacecraft had its first brush with the human race when it encountered the Mangalyaan, an Indian space probe orbiting Mars since September 2014. Using Morse code, the alien crew aboard the saucer-like spacecraft radioed a simple but universal message to the humans: 'We come in peace.'

The frenzy in the Indian media was unprecedented. From Sun TV in the south to JK News in Jammu and Kashmir, from ETV-Gujarati in the west to Kolkata TV in the east, every news channel in India was breathlessly reporting on the one and only story—the arrival of the aliens. Newsrooms of national TV channels witnessed chaotic scenes, with harried journalists scampering here and there in a mad rush to cover all possible angles.

Editors held frantic discussions to finalize the perfect Bollywood song to complement their news coverage. After much hair-splitting, Aaj Tak went with 'Jadoo! Jadoo!' from *Koi . . . Mil Gaya* and Zee News went with 'Love is a waste of time' from *PK*.

India TV was in a we-told-you-so mood, recounting all their old reports on aliens abducting cows and pigs from the streets of Gurgaon. 'Our intrepid investigative reporters have been consistently exposing instances of alien activity over the years. The other channels laughed at us, but now, it is we who have the final laugh,' declared the India TV anchor. Then, wagging an accusatory finger at the camera, he demanded, '*Kya aliens lautayenge humare suar?*'

The English channels were not far behind. NewsX held an invigorating debate on what the alien landing means for geopolitics in the South Asian region. The debate featured eight panellists and was watched by seven viewers across India.

NDTV discussed the softer aspects of the alien race, gushing about their peace-loving nature, speculating about the kind of food they ate and the type of music they liked.

The cake, however, went to Times Now. The channel did the unthinkable and actually ignored an update in the Indrani Mukherjea–Sheena Bora case. Instead, Times Now's editor-in-chief, Arnab Goswami, convened an urgent team meeting to brainstorm possible reporting angles in the alien story.

After ten minutes of intense discussions, during which Arnab spoke for nine minutes and fifty-five seconds, Times Now's crack team of journalists decided that the aliens were coming down to invade India and launched their hashtag on Twitter: #AliensInvadeIndia. Arnab duly worked himself up into a rage and recorded the first prime-time debate of the evening comprising Sambit Patra, Sanjay Jha, Saba Naqvi, Ajoy Bose and a couple of others. The debate started off with a discussion on aliens but soon degenerated into a cockfight between Patra and Jha, eventually concluding with Arnab blasting them both and then everyone else on the panel.

In the break that followed, Arnab decided that there was a Pakistani angle to the story. His team concurred and launched another Twitter hashtag: #PakAliensUnholyAlliance. Arnab recorded his second prime-time debate of the day, with the same participants as the first one, plus Maroof Raza and a couple of jobless men from Pakistan. The debate quickly degenerated into a cockfight between the Indians and the Pakistanis, eventually concluding with Arnab single-handedly lambasting the Pakistanis, with the Indian panellists nodding sagely and staying the hell out of the way.

Diametrically opposite to the tone and tenor of *Newshour* was the newscast on Doordarshan that actually provided more substantive information in a five-minute broadcast than an hour of 'news' on other channels. A wooden-faced lady read out the news report in a monotone, while another woman in a smaller panel translated it for the deaf and dumb with a series of rapid hand gestures.

'According to sources, the alien spaceship has now made contact with ISRO, and is well on track to touch down in the national capital. According to analysts, the aliens are from a species that is physically and biologically similar to the human race, apart from some differences. For example, they are stronger, faster and have four hands instead of two. They also have infrared vision in place of regular human vision. Sources further reveal that the aliens have been able to tap into the World Wide Web and may already be familiarizing themselves with this part of the world . . .'

It was anybody's guess as to who actually saw the DD telecast.

India Today saw 100 per cent attendance in its newsroom, with all the big names—Karan Thapar, Rajdeep Sardesai, Rahul Kanwal, Shiv Aroor, Gaurav Sawant—checking in. Given the limited prime-time news-anchor slots in the IT news studio, this meant that someone had to take to the streets as a reporter and, inevitably, that someone was Rahul Kanwal.

'We are here in Jantar Mantar amidst a group of animated Delhiites who are clearly awaiting the aliens with eager anticipation,' announced Kanwal, as a bunch of enthusiastic youngsters dressed as alien characters from Indian pop culture cheered wildly.

Kanwal turned to the crowd to pick his first interviewee. A majority of the people in the crowd came dressed as *Koi . . . Mil Gaya*'s Jadoo, with blue masks, yellow hooded robes and three-fingered gloves. A handful of folks came as Chacha Chaudhary's Sabu, with shaved heads, fake moustaches and six packs painted on their abdomens. The rest reprised Aamir Khan's character from the most successful Bollywood alien movie of all time, *PK*.

Kanwal pointed his microphone towards one such PK lookalike standing stark naked save for an ancient-looking transistor covering his private parts.

'How do you feel?' asked Kanwal.

'To be honest, my balls are freezing. It's so bloody cold! I should have gone for Jadoo.'

'No, no, I mean, how do you feel about the aliens coming over to India?'

'*Oh, bahut achha lag raha hai!* We will show them a good time on our *gola*. Go aliens! Woohoo!'

The motley group of Jadoos, PKs and Sabus whooped and cheered and waved at the camera, nearly squeezing Rahul Kanwal out of the frame. Barely keeping his balance, Kanwal turned back to the camera and said, 'As you can see, Shiv, there is a great deal of excitement among the people about the arrival of the aliens. The next few days should be interesting! Back to you in the studio, Shiv.'

'Thanks, Rahul,' said Shiv Aroor, flashing a practised smile. 'That was our editor-at-large, Rahul Kanwal, taking stock of the mood in Delhi.'

Aroor rearranged a few papers on his desk, then looked up at the camera with raised eyebrows and an expert sideways nod. 'The question on everyone's mind at this point is: How is PM Modi preparing for the visit by the alien delegation?'

Prime Minister Narendra Modi stood tall in the room and slowly swept his gaze in a wide arc from the far left to the far right.

'*Mitron,*' he rumbled.

The room listened in rapt attention.

'Today is a landmark day in the history of independent India. We have been able to achieve something that sixty years of Congress rule hasn't been able to.'

Modi's eyes gleamed in triumph.

'The aliens are coming!

'And they are not landing in the United States or China or any of the other developed countries. They could very well have chosen to land in any of the hundreds of countries in the world. But they chose to land here, in our *janmabhoomi*, our *karmabhoomi*, in the lap of our Bharat Mata!

'Would anyone have imagined that Modi would be able to do something that the entire human race couldn't in hundreds of thousands of years? That too, within twenty months of taking charge as prime minister?'

Modi let that sink in for a few moments.

'Mitron, this is a victory of the 125 crore people of this great nation, who saw it fit to elect a chaiwala to the highest office in the country. Later today, when I meet the leader of the alien delegation, he will shake my hand with respect in his eyes, not because he is meeting Modi, but because he is meeting the democratically elected leader of 125 crore humans!'

The room absorbed the profundity of this statement.

'Mitron, we are blessed with the three essential Ds— democracy, demography and demand. Just imagine! Sixty-five per cent of the country's youth is under thirty-five. This offers us a rare opportunity and we must not miss it. We must make this visit a huge success!

'And to help me make this a truly successful visit, I need a crack team to assist me.'

Modi's gaze once again surveyed the room in a meticulous fashion.

'Any volunteers?'

The 1000-odd pieces of suits, half-sleeved kurtas, headgears, dupattas, leggings, shades and various other accessories stared back at Modi from their shelves in the walk-in wardrobe at 7, Race Course Road.

'All right then,' he murmured, rubbing his hands. 'I'll make the pick myself. Not for nothing has God blessed me with a keen fashion sense and the ability to strike the right colour combinations.'

Thus began PM Modi's preparation for the first human–extraterrestrial contact in the history of mankind.

Three hours later, Modi stood on the tarmac at the Indira Gandhi International Airport amidst two dozen security personnel toting automatic weapons. A hundred metres away, beyond the security perimeter around the designated landing area, over a thousand onlookers and media personnel jostled with each other and with policemen trying to keep them behind the yellow barricades, as they tried to get a better view.

The prime minister wore a smartly cut Jodhpuri coat with handcrafted buttons that had the BJP's logo on them, and accessorized it with brown-tinted aviators and a colourful Rajasthani bandhni turban. Behind him, Principal Secretary Nripendra Misra shivered in the chilly morning breeze, clasping a hardbound book to his frail torso. A couple of steps away, Ajit Doval stood leaning on his left leg, right leg crossed in front, casually blowing circles of cigar smoke into the air.

'I can't see anything,' said Modi, squinting at the hazy Delhi sky. 'There is so much pollution in Delhi that one can't even make out the sky. Can't they do something about this?'

'By "they" do you mean the ministry of environment or the Delhi government, sir?' inquired Misra.

'Neither. I meant the Supreme Court.'

Doval chuckled. Before the stumped Misra could frame a response, a dull whir sounded above them, and the thick smog suddenly parted. A massive green-coloured saucer appeared out of nowhere and loomed overhead. The crowd gasped. Misra blanched. 'Maa Jagadamba,' muttered Modi, open-mouthed. Even Doval paused mid-puff to stare at the alien object.

The alien spacecraft slowly descended and when it was about 20 feet from the tarmac, four leg-like structures emerged from its underside and extended all the way to the ground, buckling slightly as the weight of the spacecraft bore down on them, and came to a standstill. The whirring noise subsided, a hatch in the lower half of the spacecraft slid open, and a flight of air-stairs rolled down within a few feet of Modi.

As the humans watched spellbound, a barrel-chested humanoid about 6 feet tall emerged from the spacecraft and stood at the top of the ramp. The alien's face was grey and hirsute, with remarkably human-like features. He wore a dark-green sleeveless unitard that exposed powerful grey shoulders. Two grey arms hung from each shoulder, veined and thick.

As he surveyed the scene, another alien, a few inches shorter than him, joined him. Amidst pin-drop silence, the two marched down the stairs and stopped in front of PM Modi.

Modi raised his right hand in Spock's Vulcan salute and welcomed his guests in their tongue. 'Kro! kkjen Yi India, R!den P!nbbarwer Qaal-za.'

The taller of the two regarded PM Modi for a moment before breaking into a wide smile.

'Kem cho, Modi bhai?' exclaimed alien commander Qaal-za, extending one of his two right hands.

Modi laughed in delight and pulled the unsuspecting alien into a bear hug, sending flashbulbs and shutterbugs into a clicking frenzy.

When Modi finally broke the hug, the alien gestured behind him, where a dozen more aliens now stood in a neat formation.

'This is my captain, Saal-fa,' he said, pointing to the alien right beside him, 'and that is the rest of my delegation.'

PM Modi nodded at the delegates before turning back to the alien commander.

'And now I will give you the most valuable gift in the universe!' he said with a twinkle in his eye, as he pulled the hardbound book from Misra's clasp.

'Behold! The Bhagavad Gita!'

Thus began PM Modi's charm offensive on yet another visiting leader.

The first item on the PM's itinerary was a grand welcome ceremony followed by the Guard of Honour, where he accorded his guest the rare honour of a twenty-one-gun salute. Before that, he had offered his guest something even rarer—a smooth ride to Hotel Maurya Sheraton in his BMW 7-Series 760Li without suffering a traffic jam at Dhaula Kuan.

Then followed a series of meet-and-greet moments. The PM, now in a dapper sherwani paired with an intricately embroidered shawl, was in his element as he introduced the

President, the vice president, the speaker of the Lok Sabha, and various other dignitaries.

By noon, the two leaders found themselves kneeling around a sapling in Rajghat.

'This place is called Rajghat. It is a memorial to Mahatma Gandhi,' said Modi, now donning a bright blue Modi jacket over a half-sleeved brown kurta.

'Yes, I have read about Mahatma Gandhi on the Internet. He is the man instrumental in India attaining independence, right?' asked the alien commander, eyebrows knitted in concentration, as he held the sapling with two hands and pressed down the soil around it with the other two.

'Uh, yes, but more importantly, he was the first major leader who insisted that the Congress party be disbanded after 1947. I am working to fulfil his wishes.'

'Ah, I see.'

The alien commander squeezed the mud around the sapling one final time and stepped back to regard his work. Smiling with satisfaction, he turned to Modi to make a remark and nearly jumped. Modi was now wearing an impeccably tailored bandhgala suit with well-fitted pants.

'Shall we move on?' smiled Modi, and started towards the exit.

The alien commander looked stunned. 'What sorcery is this!' he murmured under his breath as he followed his host.

The prime minister then treated his guest to a sumptuous lunch at 7, Race Course Road. The menu boasted of a wide selection of vegetarian and non-vegetarian fare, and was dutifully shared on Twitter by the Prime Minister's Office, supplying content for TV channels for the rest of the day.

Lunch gave way to a whirlwind of events. Modi thrust a broom in the hands of the alien commander and together they cleaned up a filthy corner in Delhi's Lutyens Zone. The two leaders then recorded a Mann ki Baat session to share mushy details about their budding friendship. A yoga session in the backyard of the prime minister's residence followed. After that, the alien commander had his palm read by Smriti Irani's astrologer.

By evening, it was time for another of Modi's pet themes—a Chai pe Charcha session on the sprawling lawns of Hyderabad House.

'Let me tell you a Shahzada joke,' said Modi, sipping on some delicious masala tea.

'What's that?'

'Shahzada jokes?' said Modi, smoothing his monogrammed suit. 'Oh, they are witty jokes on our Shahzada Rahul Gandhi that never fail to entertain. They are very popular on our planet.'

'Oh. Sounds interesting. Do tell.'

'Okay, here goes. Rahul Gandhi, Shah Rukh Khan and Katrina Kaif once came across a magic mirror. The mirror would suck you in if you stood in front of it and lied. Shah Rukh Khan stepped in front of the mirror and said, "I think I am the best actor in India." The mirror went zap! and sucked Shah Rukh Khan in. Then Katrina Kaif stepped forward and said, "I think I am the most beautiful actress in India." Once again the mirror went zap! and sucked Katrina in. Then Rahul Gandhi stepped forward and stared pensively at the mirror. After a few moments, he said, "I think . . ." and the mirror went zap! and sucked Rahul Gandhi in.'

The two leaders burst out laughing and guffawed for an entire minute, and would have laughed longer had Modi's phone not buzzed at that precise moment.

Modi excused himself and turned the other way.

'Hello,' he whispered into his phone.

'Hello, Modiji!' greeted a familiar voice.

Modi cupped a hand over his phone and said in a low tone, 'New phone, who dis?'

'It's Barack!'

Modi's eyebrows furrowed. 'Umm . . . Barack . . . ?'

'. . . Obama! The President of the United States! Your 4 a.m. buddy!'

'Ohh! Hi bro, how's it hanging?'

'Kya yaar? Universal statesman ban gaya to purane doston ko bhool gaya?'

'No, no, nothing like that. It's just that I'm a little busy at the moment. Call you back?'

Before Obama could reply, Modi disconnected and turned to the alien commander with a wide smile. 'So, have you tried dhokla?'

It was Modi's show all the way. He was charming. He was delightful. He was funny. He was entertaining. He was graceful. And he did all this with supernatural camera awareness that inevitably produced the best shots.

He even found time to tweet to his 23 million followers.

Narendra Modi
@narendramodi

ALIEN stands for A Lovable Interesting Extraterrestrial Neighbour!

5344	3323	
RETWEETS	FAVORITES	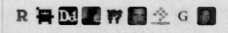

The TRP-hungry media lapped it all up. Gone were the stories on intolerance, alleged fraud in DDCA or pesky scuffles with the AAP-led government in Delhi. Modi loomed large on every Indian news channel as anchors deliriously reported every detail of the once-in-a-lifetime event. The usual Modi-baiting analysts such as Siddharth Varadarajan and Ajay Bose tried their best to write off the meet as all symbolism and no substance, but their arguments lacked the familiar bite, and anchors quickly moved on to panellists who gushed about the visit instead.

For the first time since the 2014 elections, Modi seemed to be setting the national agenda.

TWO

The Alien Commander's Request

24, AKBAR ROAD, the national headquarters of the oldest party in India, wore a grim look. A cloud of gloom hung in the air. The usual chatter among party workers was missing. Chants of '*Rahul Gandhi lao, desh bachao*' or '*Desh ki aandhi, Rahul Gandhi*' were few and far between.

Inside, prominent Congress leaders milled about, each doing his or her own thing as they waited anxiously for the Gandhis to arrive and kick off the emergency meeting convened to discuss the political fallout of the arrival of the aliens.

As always, almost everyone had answered the high command's call. Man Friday Ahmed Patel stood by the door, peering at the road, ready to run out at the first sign of madam's convoy. A few feet away, Shashi Tharoor and Manish Tewari stood chatting with each other by the French windows.

'Antipodal,' said Tewari.

'Too easy. It means opposite,' said Tharoor. 'I have one for you. Nullipara.'

'Elementary, my dear Shashi. It refers to a childless woman! Here's another . . .'

Former Union Law Minister Kapil Sibal sat on the sofa poring over a bunch of files pertaining to the *National Herald* case, cursing Subramanian Swamy under his breath every now and then. Spokesperson Sanjay Jha sat on another couch, googling on his smartphone for new articles on the 2002 Gujarat riots. Across the room, under a massive portrait of Rajiv Gandhi, a serene Mani Shankar Aiyar sat on a chair with his legs crossed, penning a poem on a small notepad:

> *A nation once led by the great Rajiv*
> *Is now run by a petty chaiwala*
> *A realm where great men used to live*
> *Is now being turned into a filthy naala . . .*

Star backroom boy Jairam Ramesh stood in the bathroom in front of a large mirror, meticulously combing his hair using a picture of Indira Gandhi for reference.

Out in the veranda, away from everyone else, veteran leader Digvijay Singh stood hunched over the railing, giggling into his phone in a hushed voice.

'No, you hang up first!' he tittered. 'No, you hang up first . . . no, no, you first . . .'

'They are here!' Ahmed cried from the door.

'Shit, gotta go, baby. Bye!' said Diggy and hung up.

The leaders scrambled out into the courtyard just in time to catch the Gandhis stepping out of their vehicle amidst a dozen security personnel. President Sonia Gandhi appeared first, nodding imperiously at the fawning leaders as she walked towards the bungalow. Vice President Rahul Gandhi followed a few steps behind, swinging a yo-yo and watching it bounce up and down with undisguised delight.

When everyone had settled in, in the conference room, Sonia Gandhi looked over her glasses and said, 'So did you guys each come up with ideas to counter Modi's narrative on the aliens like I asked you to?'

'Yes, madamji,' the leaders replied in unison.

'Good, let's run through them quickly.'

Ahmed handed her a sheaf of papers. Sonia adjusted her glasses and began reading them one by one.

'Declare the aliens as RSS agents.'

'Lean on our friends in the media to express unhappiness over Modi's bonhomie with the aliens.'

'Dis . . . discom . . . bobulate our oppugnants and def . . . enestrate the . . . whatever.'

'Meet the alien commander and make a detailed presentation to him about the horrors of the 2002 riots.'

Sonia's equanimity began to slip. Taking a deep breath, she picked up the next sheet.

'Hmm,' she said slowly. 'Now this one, I like.'

Mani Shankar Aiyar smiled.

'At least someone has come to work today,' said Sonia, smiling at Aiyar.

Later that evening, the party called for a press conference on the lawns of 24, Akbar Road. At the precise moment when the clock struck five, Congress President Sonia Gandhi and

Vice President Rahul Gandhi stepped out of the building's side entrance and strode briskly towards the waiting throng of journalists. Two steps behind her, Congress leader Ajay Maken huffed along, dragging a man in a suit and a ski mask.

Sonia Gandhi stepped up to the podium and cleared her throat, instantly silencing the low-decibel chatter in the crowd. Rahul Gandhi stood by her side with a goofy grin on his face.

'As usual, Prime Minister Modi is taking this country for a ride,' said Sonia, reading out from a piece of paper.

'He is blatantly lying when he says that he has done something that the Congress hasn't done for sixty years. I want to remind Mr Modi and the people of this country that it was Rajiv Gandhi who brought the first alien here.'

Sonia snapped her fingers in Maken's direction, upon which he turned and pulled the ski mask off the third man's face. The assembled journalists gasped.

'Behold! The alien that Rajiv brought to this country in 1984!' said Sonia with a flourish.

'I told you, I'm NOT an alien,' hissed Sam Pitroda.

'Shut up,' Maken hissed back. 'If madam says you are an alien, then you are an alien.'

As camerapersons clicked away, Rahul Gandhi took Sonia's place on the podium, rolled up his sleeves and cried, *'India mein aliens kaun laaya?'*

Sixteen kilometres away, the chief minister of Delhi sat cross-legged on the floor, sullenly watching the breathless coverage of Modi's bonhomie with the alien delegates on an ancient-looking CRT TV he had installed in place of the flat-screen LED TV in his living room.

He couldn't believe his luck. Only last week he had dominated the headlines on virtually every channel. First, that nifty little stunt in Shakur Basti after the Railways demolished a bunch of illegal shanties. That was right in his slot, and he sent it flying out of the ground in style, clicking photos with encroachers, suspending some random officials, blaming Modi—stuff he could do in his sleep. Then that DDCA redirect after the CBI raided his office. That had his genius written all over it. For a while it seemed to everyone that his anti-corruption image may have suffered its first serious blow. Then he went on camera to deliver one of the best performances of his career. He railed at the CBI for carrying out their masters' vendetta. He thundered at Arun Jaitley for sending the CBI to confiscate the DDCA report that hinted at his corrupt acts. He then finished off with a blistering challenge to Modi to do whatever he could, because Kejriwal wasn't afraid of him. Within hours, the media was eating out of his hands. News tickers that ran headlines on the raids began screaming about the DDCA scam.

He had truly been on a roll. Just in time for the Punjab elections too. Then, out of nowhere, the alien spaceship had appeared in the hazy skies of Delhi to halt his run. Now, no one was interested in what he had to say.

'Ramu!' he called.

A servant came running in. Kejriwal unwrapped the dirty red muffler from around his neck and handed it to him.

'Put this angry muffler back in my wardrobe and bring me my depressed muffler.'

The servant returned with a dirty grey muffler that Kejriwal slowly and glumly draped around his face in trademark Emirates airhostess style.

The TV screen flashed, for the thousandth time, images of Modi hugging the alien commander. Kejriwal scowled.

'*Sab mile huey hain ji,*' he muttered.

He glanced left and right to check if anybody was around, then reached under the sofa cushion and drew out a brown paper bag. He reached into the bag, pulled out a large burger and bit into it.

On his television screen, the alien commander and a few other aliens were now speaking to journalists, thanking Modi for the welcome.

'Corrupt Ambani agents,' he barked, spitting out a piece of lettuce.

'What are you eating, Papa?'

Startled, Kejriwal jerked his head around to find his son, Pulkit, standing behind him, peeking over his right shoulder.

'Nothing, beta, just a burger,' said Kejriwal, quickly shoving the wrapper under his leg.

'Is that from Hard Rock Cafe?'

'Hard Rock? Of course not! Your father is an *aam aadmi*, beta, with no *aukaat*. Can he ever afford such a fancy burger? This is a McAloo Tikki, worth only Rs 25.'

'Is it?' said Pulkit, doubtfully. 'Doesn't look like a McAloo Tikki. I have been to Hard Rock Cafe and their burgers look exactly like that.'

Kejriwal put the burger down and stared at his son angrily. 'Are you questioning my honesty?' he demanded. 'When the entire country knows that I am the most honest person, are you saying I'm lying?'

'Er . . .' Pulkit stammered.

'Go do your homework!'

Pulkit's face fell, and he quietly walked out of the room.

Kejriwal sighed. Psychopath Modi. Making him scold his son like that.

After the jazz and razzmatazz on the first day, it was time to get down to business. At precisely 10 a.m. on the second day, a team of Indian bureaucrats in crisp business suits led by PM Modi in a crisp business kurta sat facing their alien counterparts along a long table. At 11 a.m., amidst much applause, the leaders of the two delegations signed twenty-seven MoUs for cooperation across a wide range of fields. The list included manufacturing alien spaceships and saucers under the Make in India programme, replacing German with alien language Morling as the third language in schools and the corresponding promotion of Gujarati on Planet Mor, and development of sister-city relations between Surat and Morena, the alien kingdom's capital city. Besides these, PM Modi also managed to persuade the aliens to invest in bullet train technology, Swachh Bharat and the Ganga rejuvenation plan.

'But do these investments make sense considering that we are on another planet?' asked Qaal-za.

'Oh, leave the details to these buggers,' said Modi, waving at the bureaucrats. 'We only need to do the big picture stuff.'

'Okay,' said Qaal-za doubtfully.

'So shall we step out and announce this to the waiting mediapersons?' exclaimed Modi with a broad smile.

'Before that, prime minister,' said Qaal-za, sitting up straight in his chair, 'with your permission, I'd like to make a request.'

'Of course.'

The alien commander looked down at his hands for a while. Then, in a sombre tone, he began.

'You may have wondered why we landed on your planet, and why we chose to come to your country. Perhaps you figured that just like your civilization explores space in search of intelligent life, we do so too, and in the process, we discovered your planet and came over to explore. Perhaps you concluded that it was chance that brought us here . . .'

'Oh, never once did I think it was chance!' said Modi breezily. 'In fact, it very much makes sense that you are here. Today, India's topping the GDP and the FDI table, ahead of China. India is the only country with the three Ds: Democracy, Demography and Demand. When the world is eagerly looking towards India, can the universe be far behind? You aren't here to meet Modi. You are here to meet a leader elected by *sava sau* crore . . .'

'Er . . . yes, yes, all that is true,' the alien commander interrupted hastily, 'but there's one other reason.'

'Oh?' said Modi, leaning forward.

The alien commander regarded the prime minister for a few moments, then took a deep breath.

'Long ago, it was prophesized on planet Mor that our species, which was once a vibrant, cohesive and progressive civilization, would be torn apart because of the greed, venality and depravity of the powerful. We would be pushed to the very brink of extinction. And then, in the gathering gloom, a prince would be born, a great leader who would save our way of life; a visionary who would give his people hope, lend strength to the weak and bring a smile on every face.'

The room listened with rapt attention.

'True to the prophecy, several years later, a prince was indeed born to the royal queen—a beautiful, strong child with wise, penetrating eyes. We were ecstatic. We began to hope,' Qaal-za said as he smiled wistfully, his eyes distant.

Then his features abruptly darkened. 'Our celebration, however, was short-lived. The enemies of Mor, who have brought our planet to its current state, kidnapped the prince and cast him off into outer space. For years we tracked the prince across the vast expanse of the universe. We searched tirelessly, until one day we finally picked up his trail in the cosmos.'

'We came here, prime minister,' Qaal-za paused, meeting Modi's eyes, 'because we believe that our prince is here on Indian soil.'

Modi breathed in sharply.

A spell of silence followed.

'How is that possible?' said Modi slowly. 'Wouldn't we have known about it by now?'

'It is possible they he may have blended in to avoid detection. Our anatomical features are not very dissimilar. Moreover, our prince has two arms, like you humans. Whoever found him may very well have disguised him and hidden him from this world,' said Qaal-za. 'He would be a full-grown individual now, older than he would have been on planet Mor, probably as old as me, because of the relativistic effect of time dilation.'

Modi blinked.

'Interstellar shit,' whispered Nripendra Misra.

'Right,' said Modi.

'We are here to take him back, prime minister, and we request your help in finding him,' said Qaal-za.

Modi sat back slowly and crossed his arms.

'That,' said Modi, exhaling heavily, 'is not possible. There are 125 crore people in my country. I cannot spend our limited resources to find one individual who probably doesn't exist. Or exists and does not want to be found. Or once existed, but is dead now.'

'He's alive, and he's here. We know it,' said Qaal-za, a hint of iron in his voice.

'More importantly,' Modi continued as if he hadn't heard the alien commander, 'I will not hand over a citizen of my country to you, just because you asked nicely.'

Qaal-za looked stunned. Modi rose to his feet.

'What can I do to change your mind?' Qaal-za asked.

'When it comes to an Indian citizen,' said Modi, his features hard and unrelenting, 'nothing.'

With that, the prime minister turned on his heel and strode out of the room. As the dumbfounded aliens watched, Misra and the other human delegates rose and filed out of the room one by one. The last of them, a feckless bureaucrat, hung back for the briefest moment and surreptitiously slipped a stack of business cards to the alien commander.

'Call them,' he whispered and scampered out of the room.

Two hours later, Qaal-za sat facing Sreenivasan Jain in NDTV's studio in Delhi's Greater Kailash, recording an episode of *Truth versus Hype*.

'Tell us a bit about your prince,' said Jain in a gentle tone. An attendant placed a plateful of freshly cut raw onions on a stool adjacent to the alien commander, just outside the camera's field of view.

'He's our saviour,' said Qaal-za, and began talking at length about the prince. A minute later, his eyes began to sting and he started sniffing.

'. . . for our civilization to survive, we need our prince back. So we came here . . . What is that?' asked the red-eyed alien commander, pointing at the plate of onions. 'Is that doing this to my eyes?'

'Never mind, go on.'

'So, yeah, we asked Prime Minister Modi if he could help us find our prince, and he . . .' the alien commander sniffed again, '. . . turned us down.'

Tears streamed down his cheeks. Sreenivasan Jain handed him a tissue, then turned towards the camera, a stern expression on his visage.

'Why did the Modi government turn down the *chota-mota* demand of the aliens? Clearly it is an emotional issue for them. Is Modi meting out the same treatment to this peaceful civilization that he has been subjecting the minorities to? Is there no place for the needs and aspirations of the minorities in this country?'

In the next three hours, Qaal-za drove from studio to studio and interviewed with every anchor on his list.

'Is this not a clear indication of the rising intolerance and majoritarianism in India? Is Modi missing the big picture?' said Nidhi Razdan on NDTV's *Left, Right and Center*.

'Is nationalism once again being used as an excuse to create unrest and unleash hatred?' said Barkha Dutt on NDTV's *The Buck Stops Here*.

'By turning down the alien commander's humanitarian request, has Modi betrayed the idea of India? Has this government lost its moral compass?' said Rajdeep Sardesai on India Today's *News Today at Nine*.

'Is Modi rejecting the aliens' request because their spacecraft is green in colour, or is it because Qaal-za ordered beef from room service?' tweeted Sagarika Ghose.

Back in Hotel Maurya, alien commander Qaal-za and captain Saal-fa sat cross-legged on the emperor-sized bed in the presidential suite, following the prime-time debates on the 60-inch TV with great interest.

'This is great!' exulted Qaal-za as he flipped through the English news channels. 'Everyone I interviewed with is taking our side and insisting that Modi return our prince.'

'What about this guy, Arnab Goswami?' asked Captain Saal-fa, pointing at the screen when the channel changed to Times Now. 'He claims to have higher viewership than the rest of the news channels put together. Why haven't we interviewed with him?'

Qaal-za sorted through the stack of business cards in front of him and frowned. 'Strange. His card is not in this.'

'Should I go on his show?'

Qaal-za pondered for a second, then said, 'Yeah, why not?'

With considerable excitement, Captain Saal-fa ventured as a panellist on his first TV show on earth. He felt prepared, having gone through all of Qaal-za's interviews, and knew exactly what to say. Unfortunately for him, Arnab had no intentions of discussing the alien prince issue.

'Mister Saal-fa, I have only one question for you tonight on behalf of the nation,' he said, eyeing the captain like a tiger eyes its prey.

The TV screen split into three panels, the centre of which came alive with footage from the first day, where a vehicle carrying the captain and a couple of other aliens zoomed through an empty road in Dhaula Kuan, even as thousands of cars and motorists waited at the signal, watching helplessly.

'HOW DO YOU EXPLAIN THIS VVIP RACISM?'

'Uh . . .' said Saal-fa, which was incidentally his last word on that *Newshour* episode.

Fifteen minutes into the tirade that inevitably followed, Captain Saal-fa, an extraterrestrial humanoid utterly unfamiliar with the man the entire human species had come to fear, swayed unsteadily and collapsed to the ground. Without so much as a pause, Arnab finished the rest of the debate with the empty chair.

The debacle at *Newshour* aside, the media campaign against Modi quickly gathered steam and, before long, politicians waded in. First on the scene was Arvind Kejriwal, who called for a press conference the next morning on the lawns outside the hotel where the aliens were staying. With Deputy Chief Minister of Delhi Manish Sisodia and the alien commander seated on either side, and a cluster of AAP leaders including Raghav Chadha, Ashish Khetan and Sanjay Singh standing behind him, Kejriwal unleashed a searing attack on Modi, starting with his trademark coughing fit.

'*Yehi toh scam hai ji!*' he railed as camera bulbs flashed all around him. 'Yesterday, I was approached by a senior government official who told me that Modiji intentionally turned down the aliens' request so that the resulting media hullabaloo can distract the people of Delhi from noticing the good work of the AAP government.'

'*Alien prince bahana hai, Kejriwal nishana hai!*' he declared, wagging a finger at the cameras. 'Modiji, do whatever you want. *Yeh Kejriwal nahi darne waala! Aap jaante nahi mein kis mitti ka bana hoon!* We will do what Modiji is not able to do. We will fulfil the alien demand. So what if you don't give us control of the police? Our Jal Board workers, PWD workers and AAP volunteers are enough to launch a manhunt for the prince. In fact, even as I speak they are delivering him to Qaal-zaji's hotel room!'

The effect was electric. A horde of reporters and cameramen scrambled towards the hotel building in the hope of getting a look at the prince, only to be blocked by security personnel and hotel staff. The rest ran behind Kejriwal for more comments as he stepped off the lawns and headed towards his car. Amidst the chaos, Qaal-za slipped back into the hotel unnoticed, sprinted up the stairs all the way to the top floor and threw the door of his suite open.

A dorky-looking man with grey hair and black-rimmed spectacles gawked at them.

'Who are you?' Qaal-za blurted out.

'I am the Ashutosh, the alien prince,' he replied. 'I was sent here by the Kajariwal.'

An alien soldier, who'd walked into the room behind Qaal-za, stepped forward to examine him.

'The Modi only talks, but the Aravind delivers,' said Ashutosh. 'Why was the Modi and the Jetli shielding me from you all these days? Will the Modi answer?'

Qaal-za gaped at the journalist-turned-politician with his mouth open. His left eye began to twitch.

'No, it isn't him,' said the alien soldier.

Utterly relieved, the alien commander let out the breath he didn't know he had been holding.

'Thank God.'

Barely had the hotel staff dismantled the makeshift podium on the lawns, when Rahul Gandhi swaggered in with a dozen party leaders, two dozen media personnel and a hundred Congress workers. Ignoring the black flags brandished by a mob of ABVP workers who suddenly materialized out of nowhere, the Nehru–Gandhi scion rolled up his sleeves and thundered:

'This government is suppressing the voices of the aliens. Modi is imposing one idea from the top on everyone. Nobody should tell the aliens what to do. If you want India to progress, you need to unleash the power of the aliens . . .'

While Rahul Gandhi was going hammer and tongs at Modi, Ajay Maken tiptoed to the alien commander, who had come down to see what the hullabaloo was about, and whispered, 'Dal chawal or hunger strike?'

'Huh?' blinked Qaal-za.

'Do you want Rahul baba to eat dal chawal with you or go on a day-long hunger strike? He can do either.'

Qaal-za stared blankly.

'All right, hunger strike it is,' said Maken, and showed two fingers to Rahul when he caught his eye a second later.

'. . . and to express solidarity with the aliens, I will sit on a hunger strike with the aliens for one whole day,' declared

Rahul, drawing boisterous applause and wild cheers from a mob of Congress workers behind the mediapersons.

The alien commander sighed and reached for the plate of biscuits on the table in front of him, when Maken slapped his hand away and shook his head in disapproval.

Rahul was followed by Nitish Kumar, Sitaram Yechury, D. Raja, Mamata Banerjee, and a host of other political leaders, all of whom took to the podium and lambasted the Modi government for its utter insensitivity and disregard for the rights of the aliens. The visits lent fuel to the news cycle, which in turn injected the liberal community with steroids. Op-eds slamming Modi and the NDA government sprang up like weeds by the roadside, as every person with an Internet connection and an axe to grind gleefully weighed in.

'So, what do we do now? This has become a full-blown media spectacle,' said Modi, spinning a dart between his palms.

Leaning against the wall with one foot crossing the other at the ankle, Doval took a long puff on his cigar and blew out a perfect smoke ring. Misra watched with fascination as it gently floated into the air without losing its shape.

It was well past midnight. Everyone in the PMO had retired for the night, save the three men in the PM's chamber, and the feckless bureaucrat tied to a pillar across the room, with an apple shoved in his mouth. A bunch of TV screens flickered with re-runs of the day's prime-time news debates. A cell phone on the desk kept buzzing every now and then.

'Stay still,' Modi warned the terrified bureaucrat as he struggled uselessly against the restraints, 'the helmet and the cricket pads will only protect you so much.'

Modi closed his left eye, pulled back the dart and, in a powerful overhand motion, hurled it towards the wide-eyed bureaucrat. The dart zipped through the air and speared the centre of the apple with a thwack. Modi ambled towards the nearby sofa and sank into it.

'Rajdeep, Thapar, Barkha, Chaubey, the entire gang has joined the fray. With the politicians also jumping in, this *nautanki* has only just begun.'

Doval took another puff and blew out a smoke pistol that pierced the smoke ring right through the centre. The phone on the desk buzzed again.

'Are you gonna take that?' Modi asked.

'No,' said Doval.

He pushed himself off the wall lightly, sauntered towards the desk and picked up a dart. Then, still puffing on his cigar, without so much as a glance at the target, he flicked the dart from around his hips. The dart blurred through the air and drilled the apple bang in the middle, edging aside Modi's dart in the process. Doval nonchalantly returned to his spot by the wall.

'When it comes to me, the media is like a dog with a bone. They are not going to let this one go,' said Modi, and turned to his principal secretary. 'Your turn, Misraji.'

'I'd rather not,' said Misra, shaking his head violently.

'Go on, take a shot, I insist.'

Trembling, Misra took the dart from Modi's outstretched palm and threw an anxious look at the bound bureaucrat. The bureaucrat stared back in absolute terror. Misra bit his lip, closed his eyes and flung the dart with all his might.

Spinning around its axis, the dart leapt into the air and, for a brief instant, seemed to head towards the target. Then, gravity took over and the dart started to curve downwards, eventually missing the apple up above and finding the berry down below.

'Nggg,' the bureaucrat groaned. His eyes rolled back and he passed out.

'Aww, you need to practise, Misraji,' remarked Modi.

'Oh my God!' Misra cried, aghast.

'Relax, he's wearing a crotch guard,' said Modi with a bored gesture.

'Cricket,' said Doval, squinting at the bureaucrat's inert form.

'Yes, that's a cricket guard,' frowned Modi. 'So?'

'No, a cricket match,' said Doval, and blew another perfect ring of smoke into the air. 'Invite the aliens to play a cricket match against Dhoni's boys. If they win, they can have their prince. If they lose, they go back empty-handed. Since they haven't even seen the game, let alone played it, they will definitely lose. You will have your way, the aliens will feel they were given a chance, and the media will be off our backs.'

'Cricket diplomacy!' chirped Modi, delighted.

'*Lagaan* style,' deadpanned Doval.

'That's brilliant, Ajit bhai!' exclaimed Modi, springing up. 'Misraji, communicate this to the aliens right away. I'll go pick myself some cricket outfits. You coming, Ajit bhai?'

'No, I have a meeting with the Nigerian envoy, then I have to go check on the alien captain. Apparently he's in hospital.'

'All right, suit yourself. I'm off. Time to bleed blue!'

THREE

A Neighbour Takes Stock

ON THE NORTHERN outskirts of Islamabad, nestled amidst the densely vegetated slopes of the Margalla Hills, stood Pakistan's proudest educational institution, the Pakistan Institute of Terrorism Science, more popularly known as 'The PITS' in its military-jihadi circles. Spread over a 250-acre lush green estate, the campus was home to over a thousand student terrorists, faculty terrorists, handlers, ISI agents, military personnel and sundry staff. The institute's world-class four-year undergraduate programme in Terrorism Engineering and Applied Studies, and equally reputable two-year graduate programme in the Mullah Omar School of Terrorism Management were the envy of state sponsors of terrorism the world over.

Every year, hundreds of starry-eyed young men entered the institute to participate in a cutting-edge academic programme built on the twin pillars of case-based pedagogy and a world-class visiting faculty drawn from the deadliest terror outfits in the world. And once they made it through the rigorous course work, the who's who of the global terrorism industry lined up to offer lucrative campus placements. From Day 0's placement offers from outfits such as the ISIS and the Taliban, arguably the McKinsey and Goldman Sachs of the terrorism business, to Day 1's from Al Qaeda, Boko Haram and Lashkar-e-Taiba, the number of jobs offered inevitably outnumbered the students, ensuring 100 per cent placement year after year. In the rare event that there was a student or two not picked by any of these organizations, Day 2's outfits such as the Maoist groups operating in Nepal and Chhattisgarh were quick to lap them up.

These facts ran through General Raheel Sharif's mind as he stood outside the main building, staring up at the name of the institute that had been spelt using bullets for letters and grenades for the dots on the i's.

Snapping out of his thoughts, he pushed through the doors and walked into the building. He ignored the open doors of the elevator and jogged up the stairs energetically, before turning into a wide corridor on the first floor.

A series of large glass panes lined the wall to his left, providing a glimpse into the institute's auditorium. The arena-style hall, he noted with a bit of surprise, was packed to the last seat. A second later, he realized that it was the first day of the spring semester.

Eager-looking youngsters with stubbles and scraggly beards watched intently as the dean of the institute, a bearded man sporting an Afghan-style turban and a flowing black beard walked into the room and fired a few rounds from his AK-47 into the air.

'Class of 2016! Welcome and congratulations on your acceptance to PITS! We are thrilled to have you here with us on campus and we are excited to help nurture your strengths and accelerate your personal journey towards paradise.

'This institute has produced good terrorists—no, great terrorists! At PITS, you will have the opportunity to learn from the best of the best. Our faculty is truly world-class. Seven of our faculty members are Nobel laureates in terrorism, which means they have made it to the top ten of the US' most wanted list. Hafiz Saeed is a faculty member here. Al-Zawahiri teaches every alternate year. Osama bin Laden was a residential professor at PITS before his, um, retirement. This year we hope to have Abu Bakr Al-Baghdadi here as visiting professor.

'Some of the subjects you will study as part of your course work are Principles of Gunmanship – I, IED engineering, Principles of Gunmanship – II, Creative Bombing, Applied Hijacking, Object-Oriented Terrorism, Infiltration Theory, Introduction to e-Terrorism and so on. In your fourth year, as part of your electives, you will have the opportunity to study subjects from the management programme such as Terror Operations Research, Effective Hate-Speech Making, Advanced Hostage Management, Accounting and Terror Finance. Those who have the start-up bug in them can opt for the very popular Laboratory in Entrepreneurial Radicalism.

'This campus will be your home for the next four years, and the friends you make here will be for the rest of your short lives. I'm confident that you will have a blast studying here, and when you are ready after four years, you will make Pakistan proud!'

The hall erupted with thunderous cries of Allahu Akbar. General Sharif marched on past the auditorium and into the academic block where classes for second- and third-year students were in session.

'Can someone demonstrate the right technique to set a grenade underneath your dying body as security forces are closing in?' said the instructor in the first room, hoisting himself up to sit on the table.

A dozen hands shot up. The instructor pointed to a sturdy-looking lad in the front row. He sprang from his seat and jogged up to the elevated platform.

'Here, use this dummy grenade to demonstrate in that corner,' said the instructor, tossing him one of the two grenades on the table.

The student caught the grenade, pulled the pin out and fell to the ground face-down with the grenade held under his stomach.

'Good technique,' nodded the instructor. 'Well done.'

The student broke into a wide smile and made to rise, only to disappear in a loud explosion. A collective 'Ooh' went through the class as bits of flesh and blood splattered the walls.

After a moment's silence, the instructor grinned sheepishly. 'Oops. Looks like I tossed him the wrong one.'

'Oh, well,' he shrugged, and yelled, 'Allahu Akbar!' The class promptly picked it up and chanted over and over again.

The pedagogy in the second room seemed more conventional. Students sat with pens and sheets of paper as the instructor wrote 'surprise quiz' in big block letters on the whiteboard.

'A block in Baluchistan province is frequented by four polio workers. What is the size and experience of the team required to (a) kill them, or (b) kidnap and intimidate them? Assume two security guards and a driver per polio worker. You have fifteen minutes to tackle this question. Show your workings for partial marks,' he said, prompting a burst of hectic scribbling by the class.

The third room was chock-full of students hunched over computer terminals, practising a range of IT skills. Some pored over Adobe After Effects editors, optimizing propaganda videos of Jihadi John and other terrorists. Some others hung out in Internet chatrooms, pretending to be young hot girls and chatting up Indian men. The rest gathered around the handful of PS4 terminals discussing ambush tactics over Call of Duty 4 and other war games.

General Sharif walked past many such classrooms and finally arrived at his destination, the meeting hall at the far end of the corridor. Boisterous sounds of laughter wafted from behind the closed door. General Sharif pushed in without knocking.

The revelry instantly ceased, and the occupants of the room leapt to their feet. Present at the meeting were the who's who of Pakistan's deep state: ISI Chief Lieutenant-General Rizwan Akhtar, Chief of General Staff Lieutenant-General Zubair Mahmood Hayat, Lashkar-e-Taiba founder Hafiz Saeed, Jaish-e-Mohammad chief Masood Azhar, underworld don Dawood Ibrahim, Haqqani network leader Sirajuddin Haqqani and a handful of other eminent personalities representing Pakistan's top non-state actors and their handlers. A flat-screen TV hung on the wall, flashing images from NDTV. A goat sat chewing a stalk of grass in a corner.

'What's the joke? *Humein bhi batao!*' said General Sharif as he sat himself down at the head of the table. 'Please sit down, all of you.'

'Our agents in India got hold of Ajit Doval's mobile number yesterday,' said Rizwan Akhtar as the men took their seats. 'I was just going over all the telemarketing lists we have added his number to.'

'Yeah? What have we got so far?'

'Seven credit card companies, eight health insurance companies, seven life insurance companies, twenty-five malls and forty-eight restaurants. By now he would already have got calls from at least a dozen credit card and insurance salesmen asking him to buy their products, half a dozen malls informing him about a sale and ten restaurants asking him for feedback about their food or wishing him happy birthday. We've also booked a couple of rail journeys under his name on IRCTC, so that the railways can ask him how his journey was. Those guys are not even on the DND list. We have even registered his number on a few porn sites and ordered phone sex sessions during office hours. Last but not the least, we have hired a guy to call him every hour using a number-scrambling software and play Taher Shah's song *Eye to Eye*.'

General Sharif burst out laughing. '*Eye to Eye*? Brilliant!' he guffawed, his huge shoulders jiggling. The others joined in and there was much mirth and merriment for a few minutes. When the laughter finally died down, General Sharif got down to business.

'All right,' said General Sharif, wiping tears from his eyes. 'Let's begin.'

He clapped twice, upon which an attendant scurried in and began placing steaming cups of tea in front of every participant.

'Okay then,' said General Sharif, and nodded at the TV screen on the wall opposite him. 'So, what do we know about the aliens?'

'At this point, not a lot more than what their media is telling us,' said Akhtar. 'They have come looking for their prince and they're requesting the Indian government to help them search for him.'

'So they aren't invading India?'

'No, they seem peaceful enough.'

'How's that possible? Except for *ET*, every Hollywood alien movie has them coming in as invaders,' frowned Sharif. 'Are they coming to Pakistan, by the way?'

'Not that we know of.'

'Send an invitation to the alien commander. Hint to him that it is mandatory for any international dignitary visiting India to visit Pakistan as well. We'll take him to Sialkot and show him the mortar shells fired by Indian Border Security Forces.'

'Yes, sir.'

'Oh, and file a complaint with the UN against India on this matter.'

'Um, what exactly do we complain about?'

'How should I know, yaar? Make something up!' said Sharif irritably. Then turning to Hafiz Saeed, he said, 'What do you guys have for me?'

Hafiz Saeed cleared his throat.

'My team and I have been working hard over the past few days, and we have come up with a list . . .'

General Sharif leaned forward with interest. 'Oh goody, a list of new targets?'

'Er, no . . . a list of upcoming Bollywood releases that must be banned in Pakistan. You may remember that last year, after I got *Phantom* banned . . .'

General Sharif glared at the LeT founder in disbelief.

'What the f**k, man? Are you a world famous terrorist or the f**king censor board chief?' he bellowed.

Masood Azhar stifled a snigger. Hafiz Saeed glowered at him.

'See if we can sneak in some terrorists disguised as aliens,' said Sharif, rubbing his forehead. Hafiz Saeed nodded hastily and scribbled on his notepad.

Akhtar coughed.

'Uh, General Sharif, with all due respect, Saeed may not be totally off the mark. It is not wise to ignore Bollywood.'

Sharif turned to Akhtar.

'Agreed, banning a handful of movies from our theatres is too simplistic a solution, especially when piracy is rampant,' said Akhtar, 'but the damage Bollywood flicks have been causing to the crème de la crème of our human resources is staggering. Only this morning, I received an alarming investigative report on this.'

'Go on.'

Akhtar took a deep breath. 'Over the past decade, RAW has been smuggling hundreds of thousands of pirated DVDs of assorted Bollywood flicks into Karachi and Lahore via Dubai. Most of these are DVDs of SRK chick flicks such as *Chennai Express*, *Jab Tak Hai Jaan*, *Happy New Year* and, most recently, *Dilwale*. These are not movies, General, these are Indian weapons of mass destruction, specifically designed to deliver a calibrated and lethal response to our own strategy of death by a thousand cuts. These chick flicks are fermenting mental chaos at an unprecedented rate. Hardened terrorists who live and die by the AK47 are throwing down their weapons and striking SRK poses singing *Gerua*. One by one, our brainless extremist youth are turning into brainless SRK chick flick fans.'

General Sharif went pale.

'And those who aren't converted by SRK's chick flicks are taken apart by the rest of the DVDs which include movies like *Ram Gopal Varma ki Aag*, *Himmatwala*, *Humshakals* and various other Sajid Khan movies. Last week, one of our boys who we thought could be the next Ilyas Kashmiri watched fifteen minutes of *Humshakals* before shoving a 9-mm into his mouth and blowing his brains out.'

'*Ya Allah!*' said Sharif weakly.

'It's going to get worse, General. Our agents in Bollywood tell us that Aditya Chopra is finalizing the script for *Jab Tak Hai Jaan 2*, a love quadrangle starring Katrina, Deepika, Sonam and SRK.'

'Wow! That's awesome!' exclaimed one of the lesser-known terror chiefs at the far end of the table.

A dozen heads turned in unison. General Sharif pulled out a pistol and shot him between the eyes. The group turned back to Akhtar.

'And that is not even the worst news,' Akhtar continued. 'The coup de grâce, according to our agents, will be delivered by Goldie Behl in conjunction with Abhishek Bachchan through their *Drona* sequel, *Grona!*'

General Sharif sank into his seat in a daze. The attendant reappeared and gently began to massage his temples.

'This is disproportionate use of force by the Indians,' he said after several moments. 'Won't this strategy come back to bite them? What about collateral damage to their own people?'

'They are willing to absorb them.'

General Sharif brooded over this as the attendant moved to his neck and shoulders. Sharif turned to Dawood Ibrahim.

'Dawood mian, you have connections in Bollywood. Can you do something about this?'

The underworld don didn't respond. He sat stiffly in his seat, with a quivering lip and a thousand-yard stare.

'He hasn't been himself ever since he saw Akshay Kumar's *Once Upon a Time in Mumbai Dobaara*,' said Akhtar in a low voice.

'Dawood mian!'

Dawood jumped, startled out of his reverie.

Sharif frowned. 'What's the matter with you?'

'Please,' said Dawood in a pleading tone, 'can you move me, saab? I don't feel safe.'

Sharif groaned. 'Not again, yaar. What is it this time?'

Dawood shivered. 'I can't sleep, saab! Every time I close my eyes, I get nightmares of Ajit Doval calling me up and saying in a menacing tone, "I don't know where you are, but I'll find you and I'll kill you." I can't shake the feeling that he's planning something.'

'Well, I told you not to watch reruns of *Taken*, didn't I?'

Dawood went down on his knees and whined, 'Please move me to a different safe house, saab!'

Sharif looked at Dawood with disgust.

'Please, please, please!'

'All right, all right, stop whining. I'll take care of this when I have the time,' said Sharif. 'Right now, there are far more important matters.'

Sharif stood up and began pacing the room. All eyes were on the general.

'Too long have we tolerated India's provocations,' he said. 'Too long have we let India take advantage of our peaceful nature. We cannot let them ride roughshod over us any more. We cannot let them mistake our restraint for weakness any more.'

He slammed a fist on the table.

'I say enough is enough! Let's attack them, and let's do it now!'

The room roared its approval. Those sitting pounded on the table, while those standing took out their pistols and AK47s and fired several rounds in the air.

'Rizwan, call for a meeting of the Strike Corps right away,' said Sharif after the room had settled down. 'I want to plan a combat strategy immediately.'

'Um, what about the government? Shouldn't we check with them?' asked Akhtar.

The men in the room burst out laughing. Akhtar turned a deep shade of red.

'Well, let's ask them, shall we?' grinned General Sharif and turned to the attendant who had been kneading his shoulder moments ago. 'What do you think, PM saab? Do we have your permission?'

'Yes, of course!' beamed Nawaz Sharif.

'Well, there you go,' Sharif said to Akhtar. 'The only thing left is the issue of financing the war. Any suggestions, PM saab?'

'Well, we can divert some funds from our higher education budget, I suppose,' the PM said doubtfully.

Hafiz Saeed brightened. 'That has the added advantage of providing us with more dumb youth to brainwash and push into India.'

'Come on now,' said Sharif, with a dismissive wave. 'Our higher education budget is less than 1 billion dollars. This isn't some skirmish on the LoC, guys. There's no way that is going to be enough.'

'Uh, I may have some good news on that front,' said Lieutenant-General Zubair Mahmood Hayat. 'We got a very promising mail from US Secretary of State John Kerry this morning.'

General Sharif's eyes lit up. 'Go on, read it aloud.'

Hayat unfolded a piece of paper and began reading:

Dear General Sharif,

Hope this letter finds you in good health and great spirits.

Recently when I happened to go over our Overseas Contingency Operations (OCO) accounts, I discovered that we have a little over $10 billion that is lying idle. These funds are unlikely to be earmarked for any US operation in the recent future. Now this isn't official yet, but I thought I could convince our administration to transfer this sum to the Pakistan army in lieu of assistance in counter-insurgency operations in the Af-Pak region. Pakistan is at the center of US counter-terrorism strategy and the peace process in South and Central Asia, and we very much value your contribution.

Let's discuss this over phone sometime soon, preferably off the record given that it is still in the works. Let me know if there's a private number I can call you on.

Hope to hear from you soon.

Best regards,

John Kerry,

Secretary of State,

United States of America.

General Sharif whistled. 'Ten billion dollars! *Mashallah!* This is fantastic news!'

The room burst into spontaneous applause and chants of Allahu Akbar. When the noise died down, General Sharif sat back in his chair with a satisfied smile. 'This is perfect. Now it is exactly how it ought to be. We will do our stuff, and America will reimburse us. Hayat mian, send Kerry my private number, pronto.'

'That's it for today,' the general said, rising from his seat. 'Let's disperse and reconvene for lunch in, say, an hour?'

The men rose and trickled out one by one, past Nawaz Sharif who held the door open, smiling and nodding at everyone.

'Um, PM saab?' said General Sharif, rising from his seat. 'Lunch?'

'Sure,' grinned Nawaz Sharif.

General Sharif raised an eyebrow.

'Oh right, of course. Will get to it ASAP,' said PM Sharif. He scurried to the corner, picked up the goat and stepped out of the room.

FOUR

Team India vs Alien XI

PART I

NEVER HAD WANKHEDE Stadium seen more human beings. Officially, the stadium's capacity was 35,000, but on that day more than 60,000 people squeezed themselves in, sharing chairs, standing cheek by jowl in the aisles, climbing on to roofs, hanging off trees and perching on anything that offered a view without toppling over. It was a glowing testament to the archetypal mantra every Indian swears by, *jugaad*.

Never did the crowd have so much fun either. Wearing tricolour warpaint on their faces, the fans sang, danced, waved placards, cheered wildly or simply screamed at the top of their voices. The aliens had their supporters too, put it down to contrarianism or the inclusive spirit of India. A bunch of youngsters wearing green warpaint and dressed like Shrek jumped around wildly, hooting like lunatics and attracting more than their share of camera attention. Every now and then the IPL horn would blare out, sending a fresh roar reverberating around the stadium. The DJ did his bit by playing blockbuster Bollywood songs and evergreen Hindi classical numbers such as *DJ wale babu mera gana chala do*.

The cheerleaders' podium near the Vijay Merchant Pavilion attracted a fair number of eyeballs as well, although there were no skimpily dressed white women performing energetic dance moves. Instead, a skimpily dressed Baba Ramdev with two of his followers enthralled the crowd with incredible yoga poses.

Up in the Grand Stand, in the air-conditioned VIP box, amidst a dozen security personnel, Prime Minister Modi sat chatting with the alien commander. He was dressed for the occasion, pairing a Number 56 Team India jersey with aviator shades and a floppy white hat. Qaal-za on the other hand was dressed plainly in his usual dark green fatigues.

The prime minister was in his element. He conversed animatedly with his guest, pointing out this and that in the stadium, and occasionally breaking into a guffaw at something the commander said. At a calculated moment, PM Modi broke from the conversation mid-sentence, looked beyond the commander and began waving. A split second later, the big screen cut to the VIP box and zeroed in on a smiling Modi waving to viewers. A loud cheer went around the stands. The alien commander looked momentarily disoriented, wondering what the buzz was about, until Modi pointed out the camera to him. The commander duly smiled and waved.

To Modi's right sat India's Team Director Ravi Shastri, wearing a dark suit and his trademark shades.

'Electrifying atmosphere, isn't it, Narendra? The noise is deafening and the crowd is on its feet! All three results are possible today,' he remarked in his familiar baritone.

While PM Modi wrestled with a suitable response, Rajiv Shukla, sitting to the alien commander's left, leaned towards him and broke into an oily smile. 'You look e-superb today, Commanderji,' he said to the nonplussed alien.

Meanwhile, on television, the commentators took over.

'Good afternoon to all our viewers. Welcome to Amul Kool's Team India vs Aliens XI. I am Harsha Bhogle, your commentator, on what is a wonderful day to play cricket! Clear blue skies, world-class venue and a packed stadium. You cannot ask for more! Joining me today in the commentary box is Sunny Gavaskar and popular news anchor, Rajdeep Sardesai. Terrific day, isn't it, Sunny?'

'Absolutely, Harsha,' said Sunny. 'For the first time ever in the history of mankind, a human team and an alien team are taking each other on in a game of cricket powered by Amul Kool. Which other sport could boast of this?'

'Yes, what a wonderful advertisement for the game of cricket!' said Harsha. 'Rajdeep, glad you could join us for this momentous event.'

'Thanks, Harsha,' chirped Rajdeep. 'We have an extremely important event tonight, gentlemen. The big question tonight is, "Is there still a Modi wave?" If the aliens win, that would mean that the Modi magic is no longer working in this country. If the aliens lose, that would be one more example of why, under Modi, India is no longer the tolerant nation that welcomes minorities with open arms.'

Harsha and Sunny looked lost for words for a few moments. Harsha recovered first. 'Er . . . all right, let's head over to Sanjay Manjrekar for the pitch report. Over to you, Sanjay!'

The camera cut to the pitch where Sanjay Manjrekar and Rameez Raja were standing with a microphone in their hands.

'Thanks, Harsha, great day for cricket! Packed stadium, great atmosphere! I have Rameez Raja here with me. Rameez, what do you think about the pitch?'

Rameez Raja went down on one knee, placed a thumb and forefinger on the pitch and looked up at the camera with a knowledgeable expression that comes with the experience of bullshitting at a hundred such pitch reports.

'It seems to be a typical subcontinent pitch, Sanjay. Looks nice and flat for the most part. A few cracks here and there, but overall, looks extremely good for batting.'

'Yes, Rameez,' Sanjay chipped in. 'But the bowlers aren't completely out of it either. Remember that Mumbai is on the coast, and the Wankhede is now an open stadium, which means because of the humidity and the breeze, bowlers might find some swing in the air. But once a batsman is set, there's no reason why he shouldn't be able to score.'

'I agree, Sanjay. Also, there might be a bit of dew in the latter half of the match, which might make the ball skid on to the bat.'

'. . . besides making it slightly difficult for the bowlers to grip the ball.'

'Exactly,' said Rameez Raja, getting back to his feet. 'And what about spin, Sanjay? Do you see any turn in this pitch?'

'Well, there might be some turn after the first few overs. But it is likely to be slow turn, which is unlikely to trouble the batsmen too much.'

Rameez Raja turned back to the camera and chuckled expertly. 'Well, that isn't going to please Ravi Shastri one bit. But then we know nothing about the strengths and weaknesses of the aliens. For all you know they might be good spin pla . . . gluggggg . . . '

At this point, Rameez Raja was abruptly cut off because three men wearing saffron scarves and carrying Shiv Sena flags were smearing blank ink all over his face.

'Go back to Pakistan!' they hollered.

Rameez Raja dropped the microphone and took off squealing towards the pavilion with the three Shiv Sainiks chasing him and the crowd cheering them on.

Manjrekar gawked at the spectacle for a few seconds, before reluctantly turning back to the camera.

'Well, that's the pitch report. Back to you, Harsha.'

Team India's dugout wore an air of restless energy. The boys stretched and jogged intermittently, waiting for the call to step on to the field. Team Director Ravi Shastri came walking towards the dugout to deliver the mandatory pep talk.

'Bring it in, boys,' he said. The players converged in a huddle. 'All right. If we need to win, we need to play well. Make no mistake, this is a pressure cooker situation, and I just get the feeling that it's going to go all the way down to the wire. The next few overs could be crucial. We need to outplay them in all three departments of the game. So flash and flash hard, take the aerial route and give them the full monty. Got it?'

The players nodded sincerely.

'Okay, boys, have a great game!' said Shastri, and turned to climb up the stairs towards the VIP box. The players watched him go and when he was out of earshot, M.S. Dhoni removed his earplugs, as did the others.

'All right, bring it in,' said Dhoni, and the players converged once again. 'I know everyone is expecting a good result, but it is important to focus on the process rather than worry about the result. At the same time, we have to find the best solution for different situations. We have to try a few different things because if you are doing the same thing, you will get the same result. Whether we like it or not, this is the team we have, and we have to make the best of it. So go out there, enjoy the game and, most importantly, focus on the process. Got it?'

The players nodded and the huddle loosened. Clapping enthusiastically, Dhoni crossed the boundary rope and loped on to the field. The players pretended to run after him, but really just jogged in place. When Dhoni was sufficiently afar, they removed the second pair of plugs from their ears and turned to Virat Kohli.

Kohli raised a knotted fist in a gesture as old as time.

'*Maa ch**d do s**lon ki!*' he bellowed.

The players pumped their fists and roared. Then, led by a growling Kohli, they stormed into the playing arena.

Across the field, the alien dugout wore a serene look. The eleven aliens stood motionless in a circle as the alien skipper gave a telepathic pep talk to his teammates. Then, without a word, two of them padded up and strode into the field with their bats, while the rest calmly settled into their seats.

'Well, the news from the centre is,' said Shastri as he took his seat beside Modi in the VIP box, 'the boys will play their natural game and throw the kitchen sink at their opponents.'

Modi and the alien commander stared at Shastri, who turned to the latter and said, 'By the way, do you like Indian curry?'

'This is going to be a long day,' muttered Modi.

The alien opener did not take a stump guard, nor did he go down the pitch tapping here and there. He simply stood in the crease without fuss, four hands wrapped around the bat's handle, and squinted in the general direction of the umpire. Several yards behind the umpire, Mohammad Shami marked his run up.

'No surprises here. Dhoni has taken the conventional approach and thrown the ball to his best pace bowler,' said Harsha, faithfully relaying what millions of viewers had already seen.

'Excellent decision by Dhoni,' Rajdeep agreed. 'By throwing the ball to a bowler from a minority community, Dhoni has shown that he is a secular captain who cares about the idea of India. If only Modi would learn a thing or two from him!'

'Well, the Indians sure seem confident, and why not! A champion team pitted against a team that has never even heard of cricket until recently? This will be a walk in the park!' said Sunny.

'Here we go!' said Harsha as Shami leaned forward with his wrist cocked, and prepared to begin his run-up.

With the crowd roaring behind him, Mohammad Shami ran in fast and furious, and delivered a 145-kmph delivery that screamed in on the off-stump line. The alien batsman stood completely still, staring vaguely down the pitch, right up to the moment the ball pitched at a good length. The next moment, the alien's hands and bat dissolved in a blur of motion, and when a millisecond later they were visible again to the human eye, the ball was soaring towards the long-on stands.

Sixty thousand humans including the gaping bowler and his ten teammates followed the ball to its destination in the long-on stands. In the silence that followed, all that could be heard was the sound of Baba Ramdev's rapid exhalations as he performed *kapaalbhati* on the cheerleaders' podium.

'Whoa! What happened there?' exclaimed Harsha.

'That . . . that's a Rajnigandha Maximum!' stammered Sunny.

Shaking himself off, Shami walked back to the top of his run-up, steamed in once again and, with a massive grunt that echoed in the stadium, let loose a 148-kmph delivery just short of length. Once again, the alien peered vaguely right until the ball hit the pitch. Then, with legs rooted to the ground, his arms swung the bat at a dizzying speed and sent the ball scorching to the mid-on boundary.

By the time the sixth delivery was bowled, the aliens had scored 28 runs and Shami's pace had dropped to the low 130s. With slumped shoulders, he lumbered towards the third-man region.

'That was unbelievable batting,' said Harsha. 'I wonder, have the Indians misjudged the alien batsmen?'

'Shami was treated like a *kutta* by the alien openers,' Rajdeep added glumly.

'The question is, what will Dhoni do now? Will he abandon pace and try his luck with spin? The alien batsman's feet aren't moving at all. Perhaps Ashwin can capitalize on that?' said Sunny.

'A more important question than that, Sunny, is why did M.S. Dhoni decide to open with a bowler from a minority community when there was a clear risk of punishment? Did Modi tell him to do this? Did Modi ask him to expose him to aggressive alien batsmen?'

Sunny glared at Rajdeep. On the field, Dhoni called on Stuart Binny to bowl the second over. The young Binny rose to the challenge. Consistently hitting the high 130s, Binny tested the leaden-footed alien batsmen with incisive outswingers and the occasional inswinger. His line was great. His length was perfect. His seam position was magnificent.

The over went for 32 runs.

'Where the hell did you learn to bat like this?' Dhoni asked one of the alien batsmen at the end of the over.

'YouTube,' chirped the alien batsman.

'Huh?'

'See ball, hit ball!'

Dhoni stared at the grinning batsman.

The carnage continued. Dhoni tried everything— seamers, spinners, part-time spinners. Even Kohli turned his arm over to bowl some dibbly dobblies. Everything went to the boundary or over it. The spectators had the same shocked expressions that Indians across the country had worn when Ricky Ponting made mincemeat of the Indian attack in the 2003 World Cup final.

'What the hell are you mumbling now?' Dhoni asked the alien batsman as Sir Jadeja came ambling in to bowl after yet another bowling change.

'Singing *Tu jaane na*,' the batsman replied with an unmistakable smirk in his voice and casually flicked the delivery over the square-leg boundary.

Dhoni watched the ball fly high into the crowd. 'F**k you, Viru,' he cursed under his breath.

By the twelfth over, the aliens had scored 200 runs, and were well on their way to setting a record for the highest T20 score. Spectators sat in their seats, sullen and quiet, while Baba Ramdev, on the cheerleaders' platform, squeezed a foot behind his neck and contorted himself into the Baddha Padmasana or the bound lotus pose.

'The Indians are tying themselves up into knots here,' said Harsha. 'A few more overs at this rate and this match is as good as over.'

'Team India desperately needs a wicket here,' added Sunny in a grave tone.

'With that, it's time for ItchGuard Strategic Timeout,' said Harsha.

In the VIP box, Ravi Shastri shifted in his seat.

'Just get the feeling that something's gotta give,' he deadpanned. Modi and the alien commander grimaced.

Perilously close to losing his fabled calm, Dhoni stood with arms akimbo, wondering what in God's name he could do to stem the flow of runs. He ran through what he knew about the aliens, ticking off items on a mental checklist. The aliens have superhuman reflexes. Check. They have four arms. Check. Their forearms and legs are stronger than ours. Check. They rely predominantly on the infrared spectrum for their vision. Check. They h . . . wait, what? Infrared vision?

Hmm.

Interesting.

That meant they were seeing things pretty much like a hotspot replay. That made sense, because their batsmen seemed to react only after the ball pitched, probably because it lit up the spot on the pitch in their vision. And because their reflexes were so quick, and their four arms allowed them a higher level of control, they could put the delivery away no matter how close to their legs the ball pitched. That meant, the trick to get them out was not to pitch the ball at all!

Full tosses!

Mustering every last bit of his self-control to maintain his legendary poker face, Captain Cool Mahendra Singh Dhoni summoned his most experienced bowler.

'Listen, Ishy, I have figured out how to get them out,' he said to Ishant Sharma in a low voice.

Ishant's eyes lit up. 'Tell me, Mahi bhai. How can I help? I will jump from the twenty-fourth floor if you want me to.'

'No, that's unlikely to help at this point. Maybe later. For now, I want you to bowl yorkers. Six balls, six yorkers. Can you do that?'

Ishant's face set itself in a fierce expression. 'Of course, Mahi bhai. Six yorkers it is,' he said and trotted off to mark his run-up, while Dhoni returned to his position behind the stumps.

The alien batsman took his stance. Sixty yards away, the 6-foot 4-inch lanky frame of Ishant Sharma leaned forward, narrowed eyes zeroing in on the 3-inch by 3-inch spot under the base of the alien batman's willow. Then, with a Hans Zimmer soundtrack playing in his head, he launched himself. He ran in like the wind, his shampooed hair, in his mind's eye, fluttering rhythmically in the breeze like the mane of a tearaway Pakistani pacer. He leapt high in the delivery crease and, in his mind's eye, hurled the 150-kmph delivery that screamed in to land exactly in the space between the batsman's leg and his bat, and a millisecond later crashed into the middle stump, sending it cartwheeling towards the keeper.

That did not happen.

Instead, his unruly shock of hair, which clearly had a mind of its own, flopped on to his forehead to cover his eyes at the exact moment of delivery. The yorker missed its length by an entire foot and turned into a rank full toss that eleven out of ten batsmen on earth, including Geoffrey Boycott's late grandmother, God bless her soul, would put away for a boundary.

Only, this batsman wasn't from earth.

The full toss sneaked past the unsuspecting alien batsman and crashed into the off stump. The stadium erupted, and the players sprinted to embrace Ishant Sharma, who looked almost as surprised as the batsman.

The crowd found its voice again and the stadium resounded with jubilant cheers. Baba Ramdev posed upside down in a headstand, winking and grinning toothily.

'And out of nowhere, the match turns on its head!' cried Harsha. 'Dhoni turns to his most experienced bowler, and he delivers!'

'The alien batsman had no clue whatsoever!' exclaimed Sunny. 'What a Dixcy Moment of Success for the Indians!'

Ishant bowled five more full tosses that over, egged on by his captain to bowl a yorker before every delivery. Three more alien wickets fell in that over, and the rest in the next two overs. The Alien XI innings ended in the fifteenth over with the scoreboard at 215/10. Team India needed 216 to win.

FIVE

Team India vs Alien XI

PART II

RAVI SHASTRI STORMED into the curator's office with clenched fists and bloodshot eyes.

'What kind of pitch was that? That was NOT what the doctor ordered!' he thundered.

The startled curator cowered backwards. 'It was a sp . . . sp . . . sporting pitch, sir, with a b . . . b . . . bit of everything for everyone.'

'Did you just throw a cliché at me? At ME? Come over here, you prick! I will give you the full monty and send you flying like a tracer bullet!'

Petrified, the curator fled from the room, with Shastri hot on his heels, screaming, 'NO HALF MEASURES HERE!'

Out on the field, the players relaxed and rehydrated in their respective dugouts as groundsmen ran the light roller on the pitch. The Indian players had recovered from their initial shock and looked upbeat. The aliens did not exhibit any particular emotion and quietly went about their routines. A few feet away from the alien dugout, Rajdeep Sardesai stood alongside an alien player with a microphone in his hand.

'We have with us the alien batsman who top-scored for his team today. What a terrific innings!' said Rajdeep to the camera, before turning to the alien player. 'Sir, how do you feel?'

'I feel great. The ball was coming on to the bat. I played my natural game and went for my strokes. All credit goes to my coach who worked hard with me in the nets.'

'What was your game plan?'

'Oh, we wanted to bat in partnerships and keep the scoreboard ticking. The key is to rotate the strike, which we were able to do successfully.'

'Rotate the strike? You guys scored 95 per cent of your runs in fours and sixes!' exclaimed Rajdeep incredulously.

The alien looked momentarily nonplussed. Then he broke into a sheepish grin, 'To be honest, I have no idea what any of it means. I am just repeating stuff that your cricketers said in the videos on YouTube.'

'All right,' laughed Rajdeep, 'the next question is from our Twitter audience,' he said, pretending to scroll on his iPad. 'Do you think there is rising intolerance in this country?'

The alien batsman blinked. 'Uh, what do you mean?'

'Do you think it is getting progressively more difficult to survive?'

The alien looked confused.

Rajdeep persisted. 'Let me put it to you in a way that you can relate to it. For example, your innings started off very well, but later wickets fell in a big heap, didn't they?'

'Well . . . yes, the conditions certainly became tougher for our batsmen once the Indians figured out how to bowl to us.'

'So you agree that as time went by, intolerance increased?'

'Um, I suppose you could say that.'

With a triumphant look, Rajdeep turned to the camera. 'There it is, ladies and gentlemen, yet another eminent personality has admitted that intolerance in Modi's India is on the rise.'

'One last thing, sir,' said Rajdeep, grabbing the alien's arm as he made to leave. 'Would you like to know why this happened?'

'Sure, yeah,' said the alien batsman distractedly.

'Read my book,' said Rajdeep and pulled out a copy of his book, *2014: The Election that Changed India*, from his jacket pocket, and shoved it into the hands of the flabbergasted alien.

The innings break drew to an end and the alien players jogged into the field. Sunil Gavaskar and Harsha Bhogle resumed duty in the commentators' box.

'Welcome back, ladies and gentlemen. India needs 216 runs to win this match. A stiff target, but not impossible given the talent in this Indian team,' said Harsha. 'Sunny, we saw how well the aliens batted. What do we know about their bowling?'

'Well, to begin with, let's get the obvious thing out of the way,' said Sunny. 'Their bowlers are likely to bowl faster than ours. I don't know what kind of line and length they will bowl, but given the way they have surprised us with their batting, the Indian batsmen are better off not underestimating them.'

The decibel levels of the crowd rose as the Indian openers, Rohit Sharma and Shikhar Dhawan, strode into the field, twisting and stretching and shadow batting as they went along.

'Much will depend on the kind of start this man can provide,' Sunny continued as the camera zoomed in on Rohit Sharma. 'He's arguably the most talented batsman of our times and Team India will require him to click today if they are to nurture hopes of chasing down this target.'

The camera zoomed in on the alien bowler opening the attack—a 7-foot monster with arms as thick as trunks.

'Right top arm over,' he grunted in the umpire's direction as he stomped to the top of his run-up.

At the crease, Rohit Sharma gestured to the umpire, took a middle-stump guard and marked his spot. He then wandered down the pitch, flicking imaginary pebbles out of the way, completely unconcerned about the snarling alien bowler who stood near the boundary line with an impatient scowl on his face, waiting for the batsman to get ready. Lazily, Rohit Sharma looked around at the fielding positions. Then, with the same leisurely nonchalance, took his stance and regarded the bowler with a bored stare.

The alien bowler sprang forward. He ran in like a hurricane, four arms swinging, the ball a tiny white marble in his large grey hands. The crowd's anticipation rose to a fever pitch as the monstrous bowler approached the delivery crease, leapt higher than Ashoke Dinda in his pomp and, with all four arms flailing about in an impossible blur, hurled a 160-kmph fire-bolt on the middle- and off-stump line.

The crowd gasped. Rohit Sharma, however, looked utterly unhurried. At the precise moment, his bat swung down in a smooth, languid arc, and met the ball in a perfect front-foot defence. The ball raced away to the straight boundary.

'Look at that,' exclaimed a delighted Sunny. 'What elegance! What talent! Look at the quick foot movement! Look at the perfect follow through! Look at the upright elbows and the head position! This man is a walking batting manual.'

'He does look in good touch, doesn't he?'

'He has so much time to play his shots, Harsha. This man has so much talent that if he were to distribute his talent to the entire alien contingent, he'd still be left with enough talent to score a century without getting beaten once.'

'And this isn't just my personal opinion, Harsha,' Sunny added. 'Cricketing legends across the world admit that Rohit Sharma is the most talented batsman in the world. In fact, UAE was so impressed with his flawless 57 not out in the World Cup league match against their team that they wanted to name one of their skyscrapers Burj Al-Talent to celebrate his mesmerizing talent.'

The alien bowler ran in to bowl his second delivery.

'I have watched him grow into the batsman he is today, Harsha,' Sunny continued. 'Mumbai has a history of producing such talent, and I always say . . .' The off stump went cartwheeling all the way to the alien wicket-keeper. A deafening silence fell in the stadium. With disbelief written all over his face, Rohit Sharma slowly walked back towards the dugout.

'You always say what, Sunny?' asked Harsha.

There was a moment's silence in the commentary box.

'Uh, talent is of no use without the right temperament,' said Sunny glumly.

While Sunny Gavaskar mourned the fall of Rohit Sharma's wicket, the crowd's stunned silence gave way to enthusiastic cheers as Virat Kohli swaggered in, a scowl on his face and a curse on his lips.

'*Behen ka l**da, ghar jaa aur talent apni ga**d mein ghusa le,*' he muttered to Rohit Sharma as he passed by.

The first ball was scythed through the covers for a boundary. The next ball was drag-flicked through mid-on for another boundary. The third was viciously pulled to the square-leg boundary. The fourth was driven down the ground for a four. The crowd went berserk. Under cover of the noise in the stadium, Kohli let loose some of the choicest Indian *gaali*s at a couple of alien players inside the ring.

Shikhar Dhawan joined in the act, cutting short deliveries through the point region, and edging a few through the slip cordon to the third-man boundary.

By the fourth over, the two had put on a 50-run partnership. The faster the aliens bowled, the faster the ball sped to the boundary ropes. In the seventh over, Kohli reached his half-century with a murderous cover drive. The Delhi lad ran down to the other end, leapt high and punched the air.

'*Ga**d maraa lo, bhos**walonnn!*' he screamed, sending parents across the country scrambling to mute their television sets in the interests of their impressionable young children.

In the next over, Dhawan too notched his half-century, and celebrated with a twirl of his moustache. India's score was 105 for the loss of one wicket.

'This is exceptional batting by the Indians,' said Harsha.

'What I like about them, Harsha, is that they have taken no risks whatsoever. They have played in the V, and along the ground. Sensible batting by the two youngsters,' added Sunny.

'Well, they sure are enjoying their batting. The spectators are enjoying themselves too! Our man Rajdeep is out there amongst some fans in the stands. Let's go over to him.'

The camera cut to a section of the North Stand, where Rajdeep Sardesai was standing amidst a bunch of cheering cricket fans.

'Thanks, Harsha. As you can see, the mood is upbeat here. These guys are having a great time,' said Rajdeep, and turned to the spectator closest to him with a broad smile. 'Sir, who do you think will win this match?'

The spectator brought his face close to the camera and made a gangster hand sign. 'India, baby! We will crush the aliens!' he cried, prompting a loud 'Woohoo!' and 'Yeahhhh!' from the rest of the crowd behind them.

'Crush the aliens?' said Rajdeep. 'Don't you think that's a bit harsh?"

'Huh?' blurted the baffled spectator.

'Is "crush" the right word to use in a friendly match, especially when the overall atmosphere in the nation is already so intolerant?'

'Bro, you high?'

Rajdeep moved on to the man's neighbour. 'Virat Kohli once said that the crowd in Mumbai is full of hate after he was booed in an IPL match. Even Sachin Tendulkar, a man who is universally loved, was once booed here. People say that Mumbai cricket fans are neither knowledgeable nor graceful as fans in, say, Chennai. How do you respond to this criticism?'

The guy blinked. A moment later, he yelled, *'Bharat mata ki jai!'* The crowd promptly joined in, jumping wildly and waving their placards. Rajdeep waited for the noise to subside, gesturing with his hands and asking them to calm down, but the spectators would have none of it.

'Did Modi teach you to behave like this?' Rajdeep shouted over the crowd's din, frustration creeping into his voice. 'Did Modi pay you to behave badly?'

Somebody in the crowd then began shouting 'Rajdeep! Murdabad!' A few others joined him and soon half the North Stand was chanting against Rajdeep. Some enterprising youngsters decided to rub it in further by yelling 'Modi! Modi!' and soon that chant picked up as well.

Flashing a wry smile that simultaneously acknowledged the crowd's rowdy behaviour and projected his immense tolerance, Rajdeep nodded, saying, 'Okay, okay, fair enough,' with raised hands as if he were taking it all in sportingly.

Until someone in the back yelled, 'Presstitute.'

'Who was that?' Rajdeep barked, no longer smiling. He handed the microphone to his cameraman, took off his jacket, rolled up his sleeves and waded into the crowd. He bulldozed his way through the mob, shoving people around until he reached an onlooker standing at the edge of the group. Rajdeep grabbed the hapless chap by his collar, lifted him a couple of inches in the air and cocked his right fist to take a swing.

The camera cut back to the game.

'That's Rajdeep, having, uh, fun in the stands,' said Harsha.

By the twelfth over, Kohli and Dhawan had put on 150 runs, and looked good for more, when Dhawan, who had until then played along the ground, slashed a wide volley over point. The alien fielder at point leapt 6 feet in the air and plucked the ball out of its trajectory. The festive crowd was stunned into silence.

Skipper M.S. Dhoni walked in at number four and, for the second time in the day, silence gave way to wild cheers.

'Dhoni promotes himself up the order to join a rampant Kohli who looks good for his century,' said Harsha.

'Yes, the required run rate is well within range. These two should see it through for their team,' said Sunny.

Kohli continued to plunder runs. The aliens threw everything at him, but Kohli was too good for them. When he hit them along the ground, he put it well beyond the reach of the alien fielders. When he took the aerial route, he hit them high enough to avoid the fingertips of the leaping boundary fielders. Baba Ramdev delighted the spectators around him by squatting in Simhasana or the lion pose and letting out a huge roar every now and then.

Shastri, clearly happy at the way things were going, turned to Modi and said, 'He's a cool customer with loads of experience.'

Modi folded his hands and bowed. 'In the name of Maa Jagadamba, will you please shut up Shastri bhai?'

Out in the centre, Dhoni decided that things were going very well and called for the Itchguard Strategic Timeout. The alien skipper had a thoughtful expression on his face for a few moments. Then, as if he had just figured out something, he hurried towards the stadium's control room.

When the teams returned, Kohli took off from where he left, steering the first ball he faced to the extra-cover region. As the cover fielder gave chase, Kohli ran the first run hard, and turned back for the second. Just as he took a couple of steps out of the crease, his eyes fell on the big screen, where the love of his life, Anushka Sharma, lit up the stadium with her radiant smile.

Kohli's heart soared. Nothing mattered any more. Not the second run, not his century, not the match. He stopped in his tracks, went down on one knee, and blew his lady love a flying kiss.

'Yoohoo!' whooped the alien keeper as he disturbed the stumps even as Kohli, on bent knees in the middle of the pitch, went 'Muah! Muah!' at the big screen.

Dhoni stared with a wooden face. In his mind's eye, he smashed flowerpots, glass panes, the heads of a few BCCI officials and a dozen other things with his heaviest bat.

'Who the hell told that big-screen operator to focus on her?' he murmured.

'Me,' chirped the alien skipper behind him, and added with a grin and a wink, 'Twitter.'

Dhoni glowered at his counterpart.

That brought Suresh Raina to the crease, and the game instantly transformed into Chennai Super Kings versus Aliens XI.

The first ball to Suresh Raina came on a length on the middle and off stump. The south paw responded by heaving it across the line to the stands beyond the extra-cover boundary. The second ball was dispatched to the mid-on boundary with an inside-out shot. The third ball was slogged to the cow corner. The alien bowlers kept feeding him length deliveries and Raina kept blasting them to the cow corner or the deep mid-wicket region.

Raina's sixth such heave brought down the equation to 30 off 24. As the alien skipper stood scratching his head, wondering what he could do to turn the tables, Dhoni grinned at him.

'Didn't look *him* up on the Internet, did you?'

'No,' admitted the alien skipper, irritated.

Dhoni smirked with satisfaction as the alien bowler ran in again with the expression of a man who knows he's about to be mauled. Just as he was about to deliver yet another hit-me ball, his landing foot slipped and he stumbled face-first.

Dhoni's smug grin vanished.

The ball which would otherwise have been a juicy half volley that Raina would have murdered through the covers, instead pitched short of length and reared up to his chest. Already on his front foot, Raina's eyes widened as he recognized his age-old nemesis, Mr Short Delivery. His training ordered him to adjust and confidently swivel-pull the ball. His heart told him to get the hell out of the way. Heart and mind collided in an instant of pure panic, and all Raina could manage was the ugliest of fends, spooning the ball to the alien at gully who accepted it with unmitigated glee.

'F**k my life,' muttered Dhoni under his breath.

Things went rapidly downhill from there. Ajinkya Rahane ran himself out attempting a quick single. Sir Jadeja came, Sir Jadeja slogged, Sir Jadeja got stumped. Ashwin, sometimes regarded as India's best test batsman, played a gorgeous drive before nicking one to the keeper. Ishant Sharma, inexplicably promoted ahead of the eleventh batsman was clean bowled.

With two overs to go, Dhoni found himself batting with Stuart Binny, with only Mohammad Shami to go, and 15 runs to win.

'Dhoni will look to close this match in this over itself,' said Sunny.

Dhoni played four consecutive dot balls and took a single off the fifth ball. Binny faced his first delivery in the penultimate over of the match, with his team desperately needing a big hit from him. He breathed a prayer, closed his eyes and swung the bat with all his might. The ball missed the bat altogether, nicked his butt and sped to the deep fine-leg boundary for 4 valuable runs.

In the commentary box, Harsha wiped a bead of sweat from his forehead.

'India needs 10 runs off 6 balls. The good news is Dhoni is on strike. He will have to start strong. A boundary off the first ball is great. A Rajnigandha Maximum, even better,' he said.

Dhoni patted back the ball to the bowler for a dot ball.

'What the f**k, man!' said Harsha, with his hand over the microphone.

'Using the f-word, are we? When even suave commentators get down to abuse, one wonders, *yeh kahan aa gaye hum*?' said Rajdeep.

Harsha stared daggers at the news anchor.

Dhoni and Binny stole singles off the next four deliveries, bringing the match down to the ultimate equation in cricket: 6 runs off 1 ball.

'This is it,' croaked Sunny. 'Once again, Dhoni takes the match to the last ball. Team India requires 6 runs, uh, I mean, a Rajnigandha Maximum to win the match.'

'What we need now is sense over sensationalism, credibility over chaos and substance over style. Can Dhoni do it?' said Rajdeep.

Sunny ground his teeth and said nothing.

In the VIP box, PM Modi took off his floppy hat, wiped the sweat off his forehead and downed a glass of water. Behind them, an NSG commando held Shastri immobile with a firm foot on his back, while his colleague wrapped a duct tape around his mouth.

In the Indian dugout, players sat frozen at the edge of their seats, chewing their nails raw. Spectators around the stadium, no longer sitting, held their breath with anxious expressions on their faces. Even Baba Ramdev on the cheerleaders' podium held his breath in a Bahya Pranayama pose with his stomach sucked in to a ridiculous degree.

A billion humans held their hearts in their mouths as the alien bowler steamed in.

'Please God, please, please, please . . .' chanted Rahane.

'Come on, come on, come on, come on,' murmured Dhawan.

'B**cho, b**cho, b**cho, b**cho,' muttered Kohli.

The 155-kmph yorker homed in on Dhoni's left foot like a heat-seeking missile. Only, his foot wasn't there any more. With an instinct born out of a hundred last-over chases, Dhoni darted a foot deeper into his crease and invoked the power of his massive forearms. His broad bat thundered down from the heavens and struck the ground with an annihilating vengeance, gouging the white ball along with a handful of earth and sending it soaring into the sky. Sensing a red blur flying towards him at breakneck speed, the alien at long on leapt high into the air, bracing himself for the ball's impact on his chest. Instead, a pound of mud smacked into his face, for the ball was flying 100 feet above him, over the roof, and out of the stadium.

'HE HAS DONE IT! DHONI HAS HELICOPTERED IT OUT OF THE GROUND! THAT'S A RAJNIGANDHA MAXIMUM!' screamed Sunny.

The roar that followed brought down the stadium. Ecstatic spectators screamed in frenzy, jumping and laughing and crying, even as Dhoni's bat followed through in a ferocious overhead swish and a stylish twirl. The captain took a couple of steps down the pitch and punched himself on the jaw before being mobbed by his jubilant teammates.

'What a magnificent stroke! How many times have we seen him do this for his team! Great scenes at the Wankhede here,' gushed Harsha.

'What a game, Harsha! What an absolutely wonderful game! What an advertisement for the game of cricket!' raved a delirious Sunny.

'After forty overs, the three batsmen who remain unbeaten are a Hindu, a Muslim and a Christian. What a victory for the idea of India!' added Rajdeep Sardesai.

Sunny exchanged a nod with Harsha. Then Harsha walked behind Rajdeep and threw a blanket over him. The two picked up a bat each and, under cover of the noise in the stadium, proceeded to club the veteran journalist left, right and centre.

The mood was grim in Hotel Maurya Sheraton's Grand Presidential Suite. Qaal-Za, Saal-Fa and ten other aliens sat with glum faces around a table, reflecting on the turn of events.

'As you might expect,' said Qaal-Za in a low tone, 'following our loss in the game, the PM has communicated that they will not return our prince. PM Modi said that we are welcome to stay as long as we want to, but his government will neither encourage nor permit us to search for our prince.'

The room relapsed into silence. After a few moments, Saal-Fa asked, 'Can we not reason with him?'

'I tried. He refused to discuss this any further,' replied Qaal-Za. 'Besides, he has already left the country.'

They slumped into their chairs with bowed heads, unable to meet each other's eyes. Despondency weighed down on them like a thick fog, crushing their collective spirit.

'So what do we do?' asked the alien commander, a note of despair in his voice.

The aliens stared at their feet.

'Commander Qaal-Za, if I may,' said a voice from near the door.

A dozen alien heads turned.

'We need a prime minister,' said Mani Shankar Aiyar as he sauntered into the room, 'who does not impose ridiculous conditions on you. We need someone who holds an uninterrupted and uninterruptible dialogue with your people, like our Dr Manmohan Singh would have done had you come here three years ago.'

Qaal-Za raised an eyebrow. 'What do you suggest?'

With an air of superior nonchalance, Mani Shankar Aiyar lowered himself in the empty chair next to the alien commander, leaned back and flashed a smug smile.

'Inko hataiye, humein le aiye.'

SIX

Trouble Brews in the West

FOR TWO DAYS and two nights, top military leaders of the Islamic Republic of Pakistan indulged in their fondest wet dream—plotting India's annihilation. The men isolated themselves in Rawalpindi's General Headquarters and, over steaming cups of tea and swirling pegs of alcohol, stoked their fantasies of conquering India. They marked troop deployment on maps, brainstormed battle tactics, worked out scenarios of possible Indian counter-attacks and charted retaliatory tactics. They identified spots where they would deploy the Nasr missile, Pakistan's celebrated short-range nuclear missile developed specifically to obliterate Indian armoured thrusts.

'Have any of you seen the movie *Hero*?' asked Sharif, eyes twinkling.

A lieutenant general perked up. 'The Sooraj Pancholi one? It sort of tanked at the box office, but it wasn't so bad.

Sooraj has some nice action scenes and Athiya Shetty . . . oh my God! She is hawt!'

Another lieutenant general jumped in. 'I think General is referring to the Jackie Shroff classic. Now that was a movie. What acting, what drama!'

'And what songs!' exclaimed a third lieutenant general, and began to croon, '*Tu mera jaanu hai, tu mera dilbar* . . .'

General Sharif slammed his palm on the desk. 'The next man to make a Bollywood reference will be court martialled!' he bellowed.

The room instantly went silent.

'I am talking about the Chinese *Hero*,' said General Sharif when he had calmed down. 'The movie's protagonist, played by Jet Li, was so skilled that he could thrust a sword into another man's torso and pull it out, without so much as touching any of his vital organs. Ours will be such a manoeuvre. We will use the element of surprise and make a surgical thrust towards Delhi. By the time the Indians realize what is happening, it will be too late.'

On the third day, thirteen corps commanders emerged from the room, each carrying clear-cut orders, and set forth to execute them. After they had all left, a satiated General Sharif swaggered out and lit a cigarette.

ISI head Rizwan Akhtar was waiting for him outside.

'Brilliant all-round plan, sir.'

'All-round? That was just the first stage of my plan,' said Sharif with a smirk.

'Oh!'

Hud hud dabangg dabangg . . . A cell phone rang out.

Akhtar raised an eyebrow. General Sharif flushed.

'Uh, that must be John Kerry. I have been waiting for his call,' he mumbled, hurriedly stamping out the cigarette stub and retrieving his phone.

'Hello, Mr Kerry!'

'*Haan, namashkar ji! Kaise hain aap?*' said the voice from the other end.

Sharif blinked.

'*Main Arvind Kejriwal bol raha hoon. Bas ek minute baat karni hai, phone mat kaatiyega.*'

'Huh?' blurted Sharif.

'*Odd-even scheme ko laagu karne ke liye traffic police aur kayi civil defence volunteers bahut achha kaam kar rahe hain.*'

Sharif listened in disbelief as Kejriwal prattled on about a volunteer who was moved to tears because a Delhiite who was flouting rules by riding in an odd-numbered car on an even day promptly returned home after being told at a signal that he had brought the wrong vehicle.

The general cut the call, let loose a volley of abuse, and demanded, 'Why the hell am I getting these calls?'

'Don't worry, sir, I will take care of it, I'll change the number or something,' said Akhtar.

'Good,' said Sharif. 'By the way, did you find Dawood a new place?'

'Yes, I did.'

High in the mountains along the Afghanistan–Pakistan border, inside one of the numerous caves dotting the region, underworld don Dawood Ibrahim yawned and stretched his arms overhead.

For the first time in weeks, he had had a good night's sleep. There were none of the usual nightmares, and his mood was much better.

He was comfortable enough here. The ISI had made sure of that. He had a cave for himself, the poshest one in the area. He had a thin but comfortable mattress. An attendant brought him food at regular intervals. He even had a stash of alcohol. Most importantly, he felt completely safe here in the mountains amidst 200 hardened Taliban fighters.

He finished the plate of goat curry and Afghan bread placed in front of him and let out a satisfied burp. There, his hunger was taken care of.

Now, if only he could satisfy his other hunger . . .

The attendant, a bearded and turbaned young man, came in, nodded at Dawood and picked up the plate and the leftovers.

'Thanks, Aarif, food was great. Now, how about some, uh, entertainment?' said Dawood, winking mischievously.

The attendant stared back blankly.

Dawood made a circle with the thumb and forefinger of his left hand, and put the middle finger of his right hand through it. The attendant's eyes widened in understanding. He broke into a grin, winked back at Dawood and hurried out.

Looking rather pleased, Dawood set about preparing for the date. He smoothed his hair, brushed his moustache, sniffed his underarms and tested his breath. Satisfied, he put on his brown aviator glasses, lit a cigarette and sat on a boulder facing the entrance in the same nonchalant pose as in the legendary picture that has graced thousands of Indian newspaper articles.

The attendant returned with a hefty-looking goat, handed the tether to the dumbfounded Dawood and flashed two thumbs up.

'Enjoy!' he grinned.

'What's the second stage?' asked Akhtar, falling in step with General Sharif as he briskly strode towards his office.

'All will be revealed in good time,' said Sharif with a smile, then looked at his wristwatch, 'in fact, in about three minutes.'

'You mean, on the RANDI call with the Chinese?'

General Sharif bit his lip. 'Uh, yes.'

RANDI was the unfortunate acronym coined by the Chinese for Research and Development International, a first-of-its-kind Pak–China think tank dedicated to research on the $46-billion China-Pakistan Economic Corridor (CPEC). Given the amount of money the Chinese were pouring in, the general hadn't had the heart to tell them what the name meant in Urdu. That was a mistake. Within moments of the think tank's announcement, delirious Indian trolls had flooded Twitter and Facebook with a torrent of raunchy jokes. Newspapers had followed suit the next day, and soon the entire world was laughing at them. The morale of his men on the border plummeted as well, as smirking Indian commanders made it a point to make a RANDI joke in every flag meeting at the LoC.

At precisely 2 p.m., the general put in a call to the Chinese leadership to kick off the third quarterly top-level teleconference to take stock of the think tank's activities.

'Good afternoon, President Jinping and Prime Minister Li Keqiang. This is General Sharif and Lieutenant General Rizwan Akhtar, connecting from Rawalpindi.'

'Good afternoon to you both!' said Jinping cheerfully. 'General Sharif, let me start off by saying thank you for the security you have provided our workers on the CPEC. We couldn't be happier!'

'Oh, that's our privilege, President Jinping, the least we could do in return for the investment you are making in Pakistan. After all, our friendship is taller than the mountains, deeper than the oceans, stronger than steel, sweeter than honey, tastier than butter chicken, sexier than Sunny Leone . . .'

'Yes, yes, absolutely,' interrupted Jinping. 'So shall we begin?'

For the next half hour, the four men discussed mundane details of the CPEC. When they had run through the list of items on the agenda, General Sharif cleared his throat and said, 'President Jinping, I was wondering if I could ask a favour.'

'Yes, of course.'

'Um, President Jinping, how would you feel about, uh, creating a bit of fuss on the Line of Actual Control and the Indo-China border . . .'

Carefully, Sharif laid down the details of his request. When he was done, there was a moment's pause at the other end.

'Hmm,' intoned Jinping, 'let me think about this.'

'Thank you, President Jinping. That is all from my side.'

'Okay then, let's call it a wrap.'

'As usual it was wonderful talking to you, President Jinping and Prime Minister Keqiang. I eagerly look forward to our next call.'

'Oh, before we sign off, I wanted to bounce an idea off you guys,' said Jinping. 'Why don't we start a fellowship programme under our think tank to identify and reward outstanding candidates for exemplary leadership?'

'That's an excellent idea, President Jinping!' said Sharif.

'Yes, we thought so too,' said Jinping. 'By the way, how would you feel if we bestow an honorary fellowship on you? It would honour your leadership and give potential fellowship candidates a role model they can take inspiration from. You would be the think tank's first RANDI fellow!'

General Sharif winced.

'Are these guys screwing with us?' he whispered to Akhtar, muting the phone for a moment.

'Um, probably not. How would they know? Best to give them the benefit of the doubt.'

General Sharif returned to the call.

'Thank you, President Jinping. I would be honoured to be the first, uh, RANDI fellow.'

Akhtar suppressed a snigger. General Sharif threw him a murderous glare.

Four thousand kilometres away, in the elegantly designed office of the President of the People's Republic of China, two men were trying extremely hard to keep a straight face. Prime Minister Li Keqiang was biting down on his hand in a desperate attempt not to laugh, making awful choking noises in the process.

'Shhh,' Jinping urged Keqiang, and returned to the phone.

'I have another idea, General Sharif,' he said with a grin. 'How about starting an agency to train Chinese and Pakistani youth in critical intelligence skills? We could benefit from each other's expertise.'

'That's great! I love it!' said the voice on the other end.

'I knew you'd like it. We could call it Cooperation in Human and Technical Intelligence for Young Agents, short form, CHUTIYA.'

Li Keqiang toppled sideways from his chair and flopped face-down on the carpet, twitching spasmodically with uncontrollable laughter.

'Also, just like with RANDI, we can have a fellowship programme for this as well, and you could be our first honorary CHUTIYA fellow.'

Ten minutes later, when the call had concluded, Jinping and Keqiang finally let go and burst into hysterical laughter. They roared and howled until their sides ached and their jaws hurt. When they were done guffawing, they lay sprawled on the carpeted floor, utterly exhausted.

'Oh Confucius, it is too much fun f**king with these guys, man,' said Jinping, wiping tears from his eyes.

'Tell me about it. I am dying here,' panted Keqiang, still out of breath.

Wearily, the two hauled themselves off the floor and patted down their suits.

'What about Sharif's request? Should we accede?' asked Keqiang.

'Yeah, why not? It's been a while since we annoyed the Indians,' said Jinping. 'And let's also claim something else of theirs as Chinese territory. We haven't done that for a while either. Let's say, um, Andaman and Nicobar Islands?'

'Oh, we already made that claim last week. In fact, the new maps should have been printed by now.'

'Okay, Lakshadweep Islands then.'

'Cool. I'll inform the printers.'

'What are we doing so close to the border, sir?' said Akhtar as he examined the dark surroundings around him.

The two men sat in a dank, windowless room of a heavily fortified bunker at a forward post in Pakistan's Punjab province.

'Putting the third stage of my plan in action,' said Sharif, and frowned at his watch. 'He should have been here by now.'

'Who?'

With a grating sound, the cast-iron door opened and a silhouette appeared in the doorway. Akhtar squinted at the dark shape of the visitor as he walked into the room. Then the door shut behind him, and Akhtar realized with a jolt that the visitor was no man. Walking towards them was a four-armed, grey-skinned humanoid.

General Sharif smiled broadly and rose to greet his guest with open arms.

'Welcome to Pakistan, Captain Saal-fa,' he said, hugging the alien. 'How did you get here?'

'Oh, I used one of your smuggling routes, just like you advised. Greased a Punjab cop and a couple of BSF chaps, and here I am!'

General Sharif laughed. 'They still haven't fixed those, huh?'

He waved Saal-fa towards a chair. 'I happened to watch the match,' he said, sitting down on the chair opposite Saal-fa. 'The result must not have felt good.'

The alien captain's face hardened.

'This is what they do, the Indians,' Sharif continued. 'What happened to you has happened to Pakistan as well.'

'You mean they've beaten you in high-stakes cricket matches as well?'

'No, I mean, uh, well yes,' said Sharif, reddening a bit, 'but I was talking about the Indians denying us what is rightfully ours. Just like they denied you your prince, they have denied us our Kashmir. They have no business holding either.'

A spell of silence followed. Then, Sharif leaned forward.

'What if I told you, Captain Saal-fa, that I can help you get your prince, if you help me get what I want.'

Now the alien captain leaned forward. 'You have my attention.'

Sharif smiled.

'In the next few days, we will launch a military offensive against the Indians. If things go according to plan, which they will, our troops will be marching into Delhi in a matter of days.'

'And when we control Delhi,' he said, leaning back, 'I'll make sure that you have everything you need to find your prince.'

After a moment's silence, the alien captain said, 'What do you need from us?'

'Your spaceships,' said Sharif. 'I want them on standby to provide us air support at critical moments in the battle, whenever we need them.'

Captain Saal-fa sat back in his chair and smiled.

'Done.'

SEVEN

The 16th Prime Minister of India

HUNDREDS OF THOUSANDS of troops began to assemble on the Pakistani side of the LoC and the international border. Indian intelligence assets in Pakistan further confirmed the deployment of various short-range and long-range missiles all along the line separating India and Pakistan. Frantic calls on the hotline by Indian Army commanders to Pakistani military personnel went to voicemail.

Around the same time, reports of incursions by Chinese troops at multiple points across the LAC and the McMahon Line began trickling in. PLA soldiers swaggered several kilometres into Indian territory, destroyed Indian property and, as is their wont, staked their claim on the area by leaving various items such as chopsticks, super-small used condoms, burnt effigies of Akshay Kumar and broken CDs of *Chandni Chowk to China*. A few PLA soldiers mooned in the direction of the Indian posts before trotting back into Chinese territory.

Reacting quickly to the rapidly developing two-front situation, the Indian Army deployed all of its regiments along the Indo-Pak and Indo-China border. Paramilitary forces were summoned as well to provide additional support.

Then, the aliens made their move.

For the second time in a month, the massive hatch on the side of the pyramid-shaped alien mothership drifting beyond Mars groaned open, and continued to widen until it was a yawning hole. A thousand saucer-shaped alien ships zipped out of the gateway, set their courses towards Earth and zoomed through space at a dizzying velocity.

The first of these ships landed on the outskirts of Mizoram's capital city, Aizawl. A dozen aliens carrying strange weapons leapt out of the spaceship and headed towards the human settlements. Minutes later, screams and cries rent the crisp mountain air as panic-stricken Mizos fled from the approaching aliens. The unfortunate few who couldn't get away were abducted, examined and stunned into a zombie-like state.

In the hours that followed, more such alien landings were reported across the mountainous state. Alarmed by these accounts, chief minister of Mizoram, Lal Thanhawla, escalated the matter to the highest office in the country for Congressmen: 10, Janpath.

'Hello, madam, this is Lal Thanhawla speaking! I want to report . . .'

'Sorry, what hawala?' asked Sonia.

'Lal Thanhawla, madam!'

Sonia put the call on hold and beckoned to Ahmed Patel. 'Who's this Lal Thanhawla chap?'

'He's the chief minister of Mizoram, madam,' replied Patel.

As Sonia returned to the call, Rahul Gandhi waddled towards Patel, sucking on a lollipop.

'Who's Mizoram, Ahmed Uncle?'

While the Congress high command dithered over a response, alien ships began to appear in the skies over Nagaland and Assam. One by one, reports of attacks similar to that in Mizoram trickled in from every north-eastern state. The aliens, it seemed, were carrying out a systematic combing operation.

After three hours of the first reported alien attack in Mizoram, the aliens expanded the sphere of onslaught to West Bengal. The first alien ship landed in the communally sensitive district of Malda, and sparked off a communal riot that was far more destructive than the original alien offensive.

Concerned by reports of alien abductions on social media, the Union home ministry sent a fact-finding committee to West Bengal, all three members of which were promptly arrested by the West Bengal police upon their arrival in Kolkata.

The alien ship that landed in a seedy suburb of Patna was greeted by a curious sight. Even before the aliens revealed themselves, they found men and women scampering in all directions, screaming their heads off. The perplexed aliens stood around looking at each other, wondering what was happening, when eight rowdy-looking men wearing bullet-belts and brandishing country-made guns appeared in front of them. The two armed gangs gauged each other for a moment and suddenly began shooting. The goons were quicker off the blocks, springing forward in a zig-zag path and firing at the aliens. Much to their amazement, the bullets, instead of killing the aliens, ricocheted off their bodies, as if there was an invisible shield protecting them. The aliens fired back with their otherworldly weapons and, within moments, there were eight zombies in place of the eight Bihari goons.

Like in the other states, the alien attack in Patna was followed by attacks in several other districts of Bihar. The administration eventually took notice of the trend when one of the alien attacks resulted in the zombification of half a dozen Muslims. With a thick file in his hand, the chief secretary stepped into Chief Minister Nitish Kumar's office.

'Nitishji, there's a serious situation. We have been receiving a lot of reports of alien attacks across the state,' he said.

'Give me a detailed caste-wise break-up of the victims. Forward castes, Yadavs, OBCs, Muslims, Dalits, Mahadalits, plus the two new caste categories that I have ordered you to create—Super-Mahadalits and Hyper-Mahadalits,' said Nitish without looking up from his papers. A moment later, he asked, 'How much has the crime rate gone up by, as compared to last week?'

'Actually,' the chief secretary began slowly, thumbing the papers in his hand, 'it has dropped by 50 per cent.'

Nitish Kumar looked up, baffled. *'Hain?'*

'It seems the alien attacks inadvertently took out several *bahubali*s and *gunda*s. Some innocent folks too have been affected in the alien attacks, but that number is nowhere close to what the gundas would have maimed, abducted or killed had they not been neutralized by the aliens.'

Nitish's face glowed. '*Sasura, ee to kamaal ho gaya!*'

The following day, Nitish Kumar called for a press conference and waved printouts of the stats on crime rate while lambasting Opposition leaders for making unsubstantiated claims about the return of jungle raj in the state. Journalist Sankarshan Thakur promptly wrote an op-ed in a leading daily hailing Nitish Kumar's Bihar model of governance and arguing that he would make for a secular, not to mention a far better, prime minister as compared to Narendra Modi.

Kanakamma, a twenty-five-year-old woman working at the counter in the Amma canteen in Chennai's Anna Nagar, hurried towards the entrance, past the long line of customers waiting for the place to open for lunch. Murmuring reassuringly to the grumbling patrons, she yanked at the shutter and, in one motion, rolled it all the way up. Two aliens with an idli each in their mouths and four more in their hands stared back at her. Kanakamma's eyes bulged and, after a speechless couple of seconds, she let out a bloodcurdling shriek. The aliens dropped the idlis and fired point-blank at Kanakamma, giving India its first Tamil zombie. Then they leapt over the counter and began firing at the fleeing customers in wanton abandon.

Within an hour, phones in the Amma call centre began ringing off the hook. The harried call centre manager popped an aspirin purchased from the Amma dispensary next door, washed it down with water from his Amma water bottle, and asked for a fresh cup of Amma tea. His head felt like someone had poured a mug of wet Amma cement into it. Rubbing his forehead, he called his wife on his Amma smartphone and told her that he wouldn't be able to make it to the movie they were planning to watch later that evening in the Amma theatre near their house. Then, with a sigh, he sat down to put together the report on the alien attacks.

Three hours later, CM Jayalalithaa's right-hand man, O. Panneerselvam, rushed to her residence in Poes Garden and joined the long line of party leaders and government officials waiting to prostrate themselves before their supreme leader. When his turn finally came, with enviable fluency that came only with hard-nosed practice, he dived full-length at her feet and burst out sobbing at the unbelievable fortune of being able to do just that. Then, encouraged by the kind CM, he stopped sniffling and narrated what was happening in the state.

Acting quickly and decisively, Amma called for a Cabinet meeting and outlined the contours of the first of the many measures to tackle the alien menace: Amma anti-alien shields, a holistic scheme that would distribute durable shields emblazoned with Amma's radiant picture to the citizens of Tamil Nadu at extremely affordable prices. Between them, the ministers—veterans of a dozen such schemes—quickly worked out the logistics and finances, and announced the launch at the end of the meeting.

Outside, as more and more alien ships descended from the skies, AIADMK workers erected a massive banner on Mount Road that depicted a Photoshopped alien commander bowing in all humility to Her Awesomeness J. Jayalalithaa.

The first alien ship to reach Uttar Pradesh landed in a sugar-cane field in a remote village near Azamgarh late in the day, where the only human being in the vicinity was a teenage girl who was on her way back after fetching drinking water from a stream 10 kilometres from home. Two aliens leapt out of the ship and dashed in her direction. Terrified, the girl dropped the pail of water and took off across the field shrieking at the top of her voice. Unfortunately for her, the aliens were much faster and caught up to her within minutes. Kicking and screaming, the girl was hauled back to the ship.

News of the abduction reached the superintendent of police of Azamgarh, who decided to make a visit to the residence of the local MP, Mulayam Singh Yadav. The SP was shown in by the butler and directed to the courtyard where Mulayam Singh Yadav, Azam Khan and a dozen other Samajwadi Party leaders sat around a wrestling pit watching two sweaty men grapple with each other.

'Netaji, I have just received some serious news. A girl has been kidnapped by some aliens in Phulpur village,' the SP said with folded arms.

The leaders looked shocked.

'What was she doing so late in the evening?' demanded one of them indignantly.

'This is what happens when Indian girls forget their place and wear jeans like the women in Hollywood movies,' declared another leader.

The SP bowed low and asked, 'What should I do about the aliens, Netaji?'

Mulayam sighed. 'Boys will be boys, even if they are aliens. Can't really hang them, can we?' he said and returned to the game with a dismissive wave.

As he was making his way out, an anxious Azam Khan pulled the SP aside and told him, 'Listen, this seems like a serious security risk. I don't think we should take this lightly.'

The SP saluted smartly, 'Exactly, sir!'

'Good. Assign every policeman under you to the security detail around my buffalo pen, ASAP,' Azam said to the flabbergasted SP.

Over the next few hours, more reports of alien activity started coming in from various parts of the state. Meanwhile, the abducted girl escaped the clutches of the aliens and somehow made it back to her home. Battered and bruised, she dragged herself in, searching for the familiar faces of her loved ones amidst the hundred-odd men and women from her village who had gathered there. When she finally spotted her father, mother and brothers, tears of relief streamed down her face.

'Where the hell were you?' demanded her father.

'Did you go to meet that *chamaar* boy Babloo?' barked her first brother.

Her second brother picked up an axe and advanced towards her with bloodshot eyes. 'I will not let you bring dishonour to our family any more.'

For the second time that day, she ran for her life. With half the village pursuing her with rods, spades and pickaxes, she ran directly towards the only place that seemed safe for her now—the alien ship.

As the sun went down in the Arabian Sea, in a secluded spot behind the trees in a section of Mumbai's Juhu beach, Amey

Walunjkar closed his eyes and leaned towards his girlfriend with puckered lips. A minute later, when his girlfriend's lips did not meet his, he told her not to be such a tease and opened his eyes. The hirsute face of a grey alien gazed at him with curious eyes. Behind him, his girlfriend sat slumped to the ground in a dazed state. Screaming, Amey stumbled backwards, and put all of seven paces between him and the alien before the latter silenced him with his weapon. Other aliens materialized out of the shadows and together they spread out on the beach. Soon, panic-stricken beach goers ran helter-skelter screaming in terror.

A gang of Shiv Sainiks buying a gallon of black ink from a wholesale stationery shop across the road heard the commotion and hurried over to investigate. Almost at the same time, a group of MNS workers heading towards a toll booth stopped their vehicle and came running on to the beach. A tense Mexican standoff ensued between the three gangs for a couple of moments. Then, in a spirit of cooperative *gundaism*, the Shiv Sainiks and MNS workers joined hands and fell upon the aliens. After a violent scuffle, the aliens, while not harmed because of their shields, were nonetheless disarmed, bound and gagged.

As the men stood around discussing what was to be done with the captured aliens, a bunch of curious rickshaw-pullers who were watching the scene from the road edged closer to take a look. Spotting them, the Shiv Sainiks and the MNS workers exchanged a glance and nodded. Then, with a ferocious cry, they charged towards the Bihari men and began to beat the hell out of them. The captured aliens, bewildered at being abandoned, promptly freed themselves and slipped away.

Alien attacks met with less resistance elsewhere in Mumbai and Maharashtra. A steady stream of alien ships dotted the skies of the western state and the number of zombies rose rapidly, the city's famed resilience notwithstanding.

The most devastating attack, however, occurred late in the evening, when an alien ship hovered over the Times Now building in Lower Parel, and a dozen aliens rappelled down to the roof. The voice of the nation, Arnab Goswami, was about to embark on yet another *Newshour* episode when an alien rolled in through the entrance to the newsroom and, in two seconds, made zombies of everyone else on the floor. More aliens walked in, and then, together, they converged on Arnab.

Completely surrounded, Arnab realized that there was only one way by which he could get out unscathed.

'You will not silence the nation, Mister Alien!' he hollered at the nearest alien and leapt out of the eighth-floor window.

The alien rushed to the window, expecting to find Arnab splayed on the pavement below. What he found instead, was Arnab gliding away from the building with his arms outstretched.

'THE NATION DEMANDS AN ANSWERRR!' he screamed in the supersonic frequency range, the resultant sound waves ricocheting off the ground and generating enough lift to carry him gently to the ground.

In a span of twenty-four hours, the alien blitzkrieg had criss-crossed all of India except for the National Capital Region. Aliens rose from the sandy dunes of the Thar Desert and the salt marshes of the Little Rann of Kutch. They appeared in Srinagar's Dal Lake and in Odisha's Chilka Lake. An alien ship landed right in the middle of a beef festival in Kerala and sent more than a hundred beef enthusiasts running for cover. Another ship landed in Hyderabad outside Osmania University, interrupting a violent brawl between Telanganites and Andhraiites. From Gujarat in the east to Nagaland in the west, from Kashmir in the north to Tamil Nadu in the South, the aliens were everywhere. State police forces tried their best to take the aliens on, but their weapons, even when they worked, were no match for those of the aliens, and they were easily defeated.

The national media took due note of the developments.

'Was Salman Khan the reason behind Katrina Kaif's break-up with Ranbir Kapoor?' screamed the headline on leading daily *Times of India*'s front page, which was actually the fourth page, as the first three carried full-page ads.

The Lutyens' television media, meanwhile, was busy discussing the situation at the borders and debating whether the Modi government was doing the right thing by answering Pakistan's troop build-up by mobilizing our forces.

The only channel to cover the alien offensive was India TV which displayed blurred images of an alien abduction, with bright red circles drawn around the key actors. Unfortunately the channel suffered from the boy-who-cried-wolf syndrome when it came to alien abductions and the report went unnoticed.

On social media, angry Indians called out mainstream media anchors for their indifference to the alien attacks.

'Aliens attacking all over India! Mizos, Tamils, Kashmiris, all being attacked. Why aren't you covering it like you covered the Dadri incident?' someone tweeted to Rajdeep Sardesai, to which the veteran journalist replied,

'Condemn all acts of violence. Unfortunately, the south, the north-east and many other parts of India suffer from tyranny of distance.'

Then, the aliens landed in Delhi, and everything changed.

Sagarika Ghose shrugged off her robe and slipped into the clear, warm water of the empty swimming pool at Delhi Gymkhana Club. Just as she was about to push off the wall of the pool, she remembered something, and reached for the phone she'd left by the pool's edge.

'Lovely weather today. Taking a nice swim at Delhi Gymkhana Club. Cheerio folks!' she tweeted, and giggled. That ought to piss off the Internet Hindus, she thought.

Then, with a contented smile, she turned on her back, closed her eyes, placed her palms behind her head and gently floated across the pool. Ten minutes later, when she was approximately in the middle of the pool, she heard a splash to her left. Dreamily, she turned sideways and checked out her neighbour with half-opened eyes. A grey alien, floating exactly like her, grinned back.

Even as she attempted to make sense of what was happening, four more aliens surfaced around her.

Splashing wildly, she scrambled out of the water, grabbed her phone and bolted out of the club, tweeting as she ran, 'Be it scary aliens or rampaging Internet Hindu trolls, we should not cow down! Keep fighting, tweeple!'

In the next few hours, more than a hundred alien ships descended on Delhi's Lutyens Zone. Thousands of alien soldiers fanned out and took control of the Parliament, the Central Secretariat, the embassies, the iconic India Gate,

Khan Market and all other prominent spots. With the army unavailable and the police force busy dealing with an AAP protest, the aliens faced no resistance whatsoever.

With his hold over the national capital absolute, alien commander Qaal-za sauntered into 7, Race Course Road, slid the door sign outside the bungalow from 'Out' to 'In' and pushed the front door open. Then he turned around, smiled at Captain Saal-fa, and said, 'Say hi to Prime Minister Qaal-za.'

Captain Saal-fa and the alien soldiers behind him kneeled, and India had its sixteenth prime minister.

Home Minister Rajnath Singh ripped out the last remaining hair from his head in frustration and looked around the room at the members of the Cabinet Committee on Security.

'Where the hell is Ajit Doval?'

Sushma Swaraj, Manohar Parrikar and Arun Jaitley glanced at each other and shrugged.

Rajnath massaged his forehead. With all hell breaking loose in the Lutyens Zone, the committee had decided to avoid South Block and had gathered in a sleazy DDA apartment in Janakpuri instead.

'Okay, shit seems to have hit the fan. What do we do?' he asked.

'Well, our army is equipped to fight a two-front war, not a three-front one,' said Parrikar. 'So, while our forces will handle Pakistan and China, when it comes to the aliens, we are on our own.'

'Hmm,' said Rajnath. 'Any suggestions?'

The ministers shrugged once again.

Rajnath sighed.

'Let's call Modiji.'

On an island in the Pacific Ocean, 9400 kilometres away, Modi beamed at Manasseh Sogavare, the prime minister of Solomon Islands, and yanked him into a tight hug. Still wrapped in the embrace, he slid open his smartphone and ticked off 'Prime Minister of Solomon Islands' on a list titled 'Bucket list of hugs'.

When Modi finally released the wriggling Sogavare, an aide came up to him and whispered something in his ear. Modi's smile vanished. Without so much as a farewell gesture to poor Sogavare, he swung around and made straight for Air India One.

EIGHT

The Dark Knight

ALIEN COMMANDER QAAL-ZA'S first decision as the prime minister of India was inspired from one of the tallest icons of the Congress party. Invoking Article 352, Qaal-za declared a National Emergency in the country on account of the threat to its security from external aggressors, i.e. the aliens. The alien commander then pulled another leaf out of Indira Gandhi's book and began sending out his soldiers to capture and jail political leaders in Delhi.

In line with the nation's founding principles, the operation was secular and non-discriminating. MPs, MLAs and office-holders, irrespective of party affiliations and ideologies, were picked up from all over the city. Dozens of ministers were picked up from government offices in the Central Secretariat. Piyush Goyal, Suresh Prabhu, Sushma Swaraj, Nirmala Sitharaman, Dharmendra Pradhan, Rajnath Singh, Manohar Parrikar and several other leaders who had diligently turned up for work were captured. Nitin Gadkari escaped the aliens briefly, only to be picked up later from a nearby samosa stand. Scores of BJP MPs were hauled up from the party's headquarters on Ashoka Road. Shatrughan Sinha was arrested when he went to meet the alien commander to congratulate him and tell him that he would be good for India. AAP MLAs who weren't already in jail were reunited with their colleagues in prison. Left leaders were apprehended from the JNU campus. TRS and TDP MPs were grabbed from the mess in Andhra Bhavan.

The aliens didn't spare even the Margdarshak Mandal.

'Come on, man! Why are you taking us? We are utterly irrelevant in today's politics!' cried Murli Manohar Joshi as a couple of aliens hauled him away.

Behind him, dragged along by another two aliens, L.K. Advani exclaimed triumphantly, 'Didn't I tell you that Emergency will return?'

Not all political leaders were caught, though. The slippery ones escaped the clutches of the alien soldiers.

Six aliens entered Kejriwal's residence through the front door. The CM was busy in his home office reviewing the week's Bollywood releases when he heard a loud noise outside the room. He stepped out to find five aliens standing in his living room, and one lying spread-eagled in a pool of raita.

'Coward Modi sent you here to raid my home office, didn't he? The psychopath told you to grab the committee report on my desk that exposes Arun Jaitley's blatant corruption, didn't he?' he demanded angrily.

The aliens lunged at him. Unfortunately, in their enthusiasm, they ignored the puddles of spilled raita all over the house. One by one, they slipped and tumbled and landed hard on their extraterrestrial posteriors. Kejriwal, on the other hand, yanked the muffler from around his neck, hooked one end through a ring on the ceiling and swung from room to room like Tarzan in the jungle all the way to the bungalow's back entrance, and escaped into the traffic.

An alien unit entered Rashtrapati Bhavan to nab the President. By the time they were halfway through searching the 340 rooms in the mansion, two aliens had lost their way, never to be seen again. The rest gave up the search and returned empty-handed.

A few kilometres away, two dozen aliens surrounded the 10, Janpath compound. Watching them stand at the gate, a bunch of Congress leaders formed a human chain in front of the building's entrance.

'I will even shoot for Soniaji,' declared Sushil Kumar Shinde.

'*Aliens, tum 10, Janpath aa toh gaye, ab waapas kaise jaoge!*' bellowed Salman Khurshid.

The moment the aliens walked through the gate, the human chain ruptured and the leaders ran helter-skelter. Some were captured, some others managed to escape. Two aliens barged into the building, looking for the Gandhis. All they found was a leftover slice of pizza and a Chhota Bheem action figure.

'Maa Jagadamba!' cried Modi. 'I don't believe this! You're telling me that after just two years, I have to fight all over again to become the PM?'

Amit Shah stood with his head bowed as a visibly annoyed Modi stomped around the room.

Two hours earlier, Air India One had landed in an unused runway adjacent to the international airport. Shah, who was there to receive his boss, ushered him into a non-descript car and then drove him to Gujarat Bhavan using a circuitous route to avoid the aliens.

'Let me talk to Qaal-za,' said Modi after several moments. 'Ring the landline at 7, RCR.'

Shah dialled the number on the phone by the couch and handed Modi the wireless handset. 'You have to cut the call after thirty seconds, Modi bhai, so that he doesn't trace our location.'

Modi nodded and held the handset against his ear.

'Hello?' said Qaal-za.

'Hello, Qaal-za bhai, this is Modi.'

A sound of villainous laughter rang out at the other end.

'Qaal-za bhai, what is all this?' asked Modi in a tone full of compassion and understanding. 'Why did you do this?'

Qaal-za continued to laugh.

'I now understand how much you miss your prince. Sometimes I too miss my mother so much,' sniffed Modi. 'I promise you, the first thing I'll do after I get back to 7, RCR is set up a high-powered committee under the leadership of a Cabinet minister. We'll launch a nationwide campaign called "Search in India" under which . . .'

'It's a little late for all that, Modiji,' said Qaal-za, '*I* will be setting up the committees and launching the campaigns now, not you.'

Modi was silent for a moment.

'This will never work, Qaal-za bhai. The people of India will not tolerate this.'

'I don't think so, Modiji. Your media is already hailing this change. Check out this headline by one of your media houses: Major blow to Modi as secular aliens overthrow Hindu nationalist government to usher in new egalitarian era,' said Qaal-za, a grin in his voice. 'Tonight, I have a series of exclusive interviews lined up, with Rajdeep, Barkha, Karan Thapar, all of whom will rave about me and my secular credentials. I'll pick something nice to wear from your walk-in wardrobe, which is now *my* walk-in wardrobe,' chuckled Qaal-za.

Modi did not say anything.

'Tomorrow I'll hold a meeting of the MPs, who, by the way, are all my people now. I'll bend down on the Parliament stairs and touch the carpeted steps with my forehead. Then, I'll pass the GST bill in my very first session.'

Still Modi kept mum.

'Oh, next week, I'm planning to visit the US on Barack's invitation. We had a chat on the hotline earlier today and we got along really well. After that I'll go to the UK, Japan, Russia, Brazil, China . . .'

'YOU WILL PAY FOR THIS, QAAL-ZA!' Modi screamed.

The wicked laughter that followed was cut short by Shah.

'Uh, thirty seconds up, Modi bhai,' he murmured, looking fearfully at his apoplectic boss.

Modi looked like he was about to explode. His eyes were bloodshot, his nostrils were flaring, his entire body was trembling. Abruptly, he sat down in a pranic pose and began to meditate. After about a minute, during which his breathing gradually returned to normal, he opened his eyes.

'I need my advisers,' he said.

Modi eyed the Type VIII bungalow across the street, from his vantage point behind the jamun tree. With a quick glance at either side of the road, he dashed across the street and slipped behind another jamun tree. With another furtive glance around him, he hoisted himself over the compound wall, then tiptoed to the bungalow's front door, and rang the bell.

Moments later, the door opened by a few inches and Misra's face popped up in the gap.

'Yes?' he said haughtily.

'We need to talk, Misraji, but not here. Come on, let's go!' said Modi.

'This is not the time. Please take an appointment with the office and come see me during regular hours,' Misra said brusquely and began closing the door.

Modi stuck his foot through the gap.

'What the hell, Misraji? Why are you going all babu on me?' he hissed. 'And what are you doing here at home, instead of fighting against the aliens? Don't you want things to go back to normal? Don't you want your job back?'

'I still have mine. I'm principal secretary to Honourable Prime Minister Qaal-za.'

'What?!' blurted Modi, aghast.

Misra's demeanour turned meek.

'Please Modiji,' he pleaded. 'I'm just a bureaucrat. You know how we are.'

After glaring at the principal secretary for a couple of seconds, Modi gave in and stepped back, upon which Misra quickly shut the door and bolted it.

His attempts to enlist other senior bureaucrats met with similar results. His luck with Doval was even worse. He couldn't even locate the NSA, let alone communicate with him.

'Perhaps he got caught by the aliens,' Shah suggested unhelpfully.

'Hmm,' intoned Modi, rubbing his forehead.

'What do we do now?'

Modi sighed heavily.

'Time to scrape the bottom of the barrel. Call for a party meeting.'

Sonia Gandhi pulled the pallu of her saree over her head and waited nervously in the boarding area of Indira Gandhi International Airport's Terminal 3. Beside her, Rahul Gandhi played with a rubber ball, gleefully bouncing it off the seat in front of him again and again.

'Ladies and gentlemen,' said the announcer, 'Alitalia announces the boarding of its flight AZ-7039. Passengers travelling with infants are requested to board the flight first.'

Sonia Gandhi exhaled in relief and rose to her feet. 'Come on, beta, time to go.'

Holding on tightly to Rahul's wrist, she pushed through the crowd to the top of the line, got the boarding passes verified and sprinted along the aerobridge.

Just a few more minutes, she thought, and we'll be safely on our way out of this country.

That's when she spotted the alien soldier standing at the end of the bridge, scrutinizing passengers as they stepped into the plane. In a panic, she skidded to an abrupt halt, turned around and began running in the other direction. The commotion alerted the alien soldier on the bridge, who immediately recognized the two leaders and promptly sounded an alert on his walkie-talkie. Within minutes, scores of aliens spread out in the airport, hunting for the two runaways.

Surrounded by aliens in all directions, Sonia dashed out of the gate into the open area. Using every ounce of the pluck she had demonstrated as the leader of a party that ran India for over sixty years, she dodged her chasers, running through the parking zone, across the taxiways, and into the hangar area. When she realized that she had outrun all of them, she decided it was time to hide. She stopped to catch her breath and scanned the space around her. A hundred metres from where they stood glistened the massive form of the alien spaceship Qaal-za had come in. Realizing that the saucer-shaped spaceship would be the last place the aliens would look in, she grabbed Rahul's arm and ran towards it.

The meeting of BJP MPs and leaders at the RSS office in Jhandewalan started on a sombre note as party leaders who had managed to evade the aliens thus far quietly filed in one by one and occupied the seats around the circular table. Modi was already seated at the table, flanked by RSS chief Mohan Bhagwat on one side and Arun Jaitley on the other. Shah sat next to Bhagwat.

A cow tethered to a post in the corner watched the proceedings with a placid expression. Yogi Adityanath knelt between its legs, expertly milking the bovine animal, while Sakshi Maharaj squatted a couple of feet behind, diligently scraping a pile of cow dung into a bowl.

When the trickle of people stopped and it looked like no more would come, Modi began.

'So what do we do now? The situation is really worrisome.'

'Not really, Modi bhai,' said Arun Jaitley. 'The fundamentals of the Indian economy are strong. Obviously, the turbulence in global markets will impact India, but the effect is transient . . .'

'I'm talking about the aliens, Arunji,' snapped Modi.

'Oh,' said Jaitley. 'Yes, I appeal to them to stop this politics of obstructionism. India stands at the cusp of a historic opportunity to grow at a fast pace at a time when China and others are slowing down. Petty politics should not be allowed to squander this opportunity.'

Modi groaned.

'Anyone else? Speak freely.'

'We should ask the aliens to quit Bharat and go to Pakistan,' said Sadhvi Niranjan Jyoti.

'I agree,' piped Yogi Adityanath, peeping out from underneath the cow's udders, 'or Afghanistan for that matter.'

'Technically they would still be in Akhand Bharat, though,' pointed out Bhagwat.

'I think we must ask all Hindu women to produce more children to counter the growing number of aliens and zombies in India,' said Sakshi Maharaj.

Modi looked from Sadhvi Jyoti to Yogi Adityanath to the grinning Sakshi Maharaj and ground his teeth to keep a lid on his frustration. He looked around the room, searching for a face he could turn to for some good advice. He failed. The aliens had taken the few good people he had and left him with a bunch of jokers. Left with no option, he turned reluctantly towards Jaitley, only to find his chair empty.

'Where did he go?' he exclaimed.

As if in answer, Jaitley's voice wafted in from over his shoulder.

'Barkha, the alien invasion is definitely a concern for this government. Let me assure you that we are working hard to resolve . . .'

For a moment, Modi looked gobsmacked. Then, he caught the stares of the people sitting opposite him and followed their line of sight to the flat-screen TV behind him, where the finance minister was chatting with Barkha Dutt in an NDTV live exclusive.

'How . . . ?' he sputtered.

A moment later, his shoulders slumped in defeat.

'Um, okay, that's all for today I guess, thank you for your ideas,' he said in a resigned tone.

Bhagwat took over.

'Okay then. So shall we finish the meeting in customary fashion?' he asked, beaming around the room, before yelling, *'Bharat mata ki . . . ?'*

'JAI!' the leaders in the room hollered back.

'Bharat mata ki . . . ?'

'JAI!'

For one whole minute, the leaders voiced their full-throated love for mother India. Unfortunately, the ensuing din attracted the attention of a unit of alien soldiers passing by, and they came over to investigate. Spotting several humans in the room who were on their wanted list, the aliens crashed through the windows in a front roll, sprang to their feet and fired into the air.

'All of you surrender!' cried one of them.

While most of the rays from the aliens' guns were absorbed by the ceiling, one caught a piece of mirror on the chandelier and ricocheted on to the unsuspecting cow.

The cow's eyes rolled upwards and it slumped to the ground with its mouth half-open.

Sakshi Maharaj and Yogi Adityanath's eyes widened in horror. With an ear-splitting scream, they sprang towards the aliens with raised fists. A dozen others including Bhagwat followed, leading to a mini riot.

Amidst the ruckus, Modi and Shah sneaked out through the door and took off running into the streets, unnoticed by the aliens who were busy firing at the others. After running for several minutes, they realized they were not being chased, and collapsed to the ground, panting heavily.

'God, we suck!' said Modi, when he finally caught his breath.

Shah, still panting, only nodded.

The two huffed and puffed for a few minutes. When they had recovered, Modi rose to his feet.

'Now there's only one man who can help us,' he said grimly, his jaw set.

'Who?' asked Shah.

'The hero we deserve, and also the one we need right now. A not-so-silent guardian, a watchful protector, our dark knight.'

In the dark of the moonless night, hidden from the eyes of patrolling alien soldiers, Modi and Shah darted into the compound of the second most powerful court in India after *Newshour*: the Supreme Court. Using ropes and vacuum gloves, the two men scaled the northern walls, all the way to the roof, and pulled themselves over the parapet wall. Without stopping to rest, they sprinted along the edge keeping a low profile, until they reached the foot of the tallest dome of the building.

Shah threw a quick look around him, then switched on a small torch and directed the beam on to a side of the dome. Hidden there under the shadow of a ledge, was a switch.

'Here goes,' said Modi, and flipped the switch.

A metallic twang sounded in the still night air and a powerful searchlight fastened to the tip of the dome switched on. From the searchlight, a bright beam of light trailed high into the sky and shone a white shadow on the clouds. Silhouetted on that shadow was the unmistakable symbol of 'Om'.

'You looking for me?' said a distinctively gruff voice behind Shah.

Startled, Shah dropped the torch and spun around. A shadowy figure stood in the darkness, grim and foreboding, his cape fluttering about him.

Shah's mouth dropped open.

'Batman?' he gaped, his voice quavering.

The figure stepped forward into the light of the torch lying on the ground.

'No, you dumbo. It's me. I just have a bad cold,' said Subramanian Swamy, gathering his billowing dhoti around him.

'How did you get here so soon?' asked Modi, bewildered. 'We didn't even see you coming.'

'Oh, I have taken to sleeping here on the terrace. Saves me the daily commute to and from the Supreme Court.'

Modi nodded.

There was then an awkward silence.

'Swamyji . . .' he hesitated.

Swamy raised a hand. 'Say no more. Come on, let's nail ET and his alien *porki* reptiles.'

And thus, the human fightback against the aliens began.

When dawn broke the following day, the notification light on Qaal-za's phone was blinking. The alien commander swiped the phone screen and clicked on the video message in his inbox from a sender named 'The Virat Hindu'. What came next sent a very human chill down the alien's spine.

'ET,' said Subramanian Swamy in a tone dripping with menace, 'there is still time. Confess to your crimes in court, apologize to this nation and publicly accept your Hindu ancestry. If you do this, I'll consider sparing you. Else, you will go to Tihar jail just like TDK, PC and Robber.'

NINE

The Plan

'MY MASTERPLAN TO overthrow the alien rascals consists of three steps,' said Swamy as he fiddled with the rusty padlock on the door. The three men stood outside an unremarkable apartment in a lower-middle-class colony in Punjabi Bagh.

'. . . and the second step is to find a place that we can use as our headquarters to perform the third step, which is to plan and execute our counter-attack on ET.'

Swamy swung the door open and walked into an unswept but spacious living room. 'This is the apartment I stayed in when I went underground during the Emergency. It should serve as our headquarters.'

'Wait a minute,' said Shah as he followed Swamy in. 'What's the first step?'

'First step is to fix an abbreviation for our enemy Qaal-za,' Swamy replied impatiently, 'which I have already done. It's "ET".'

'Oh.'

Modi gave the apartment a once-over and nodded appreciatively, 'Nice place, Swamyji,' he said. 'What's next?'

Swamy flashed a confident smile. 'Research.'

Twelve hours later, the three men rubbed their eyes wearily. Between them, they had binge-watched more than a dozen alien invasion movies, including *Independence Day*, *Mars Attacks!*, *War of the Worlds*, *The Host*, *Pacific Rim*, *The Day the Earth Stood Still*, *Cowboys and Aliens* and several others. However, they were no closer to formulating a strategy to take on the aliens.

'What's next?' asked Modi.

Shah riffled through a pile of DVDs. 'Uh, next, we have the *Transformers* series.'

Modi groaned. 'Like that will help us. How do you fight the nasty aliens? Find some good aliens and get them to fight the nasty ones!' he said sarcastically. 'This is going nowhere.'

'Yeah,' said Shah gloomily, sinking back in his seat.

While the two men sulked, Swamy, who had been unusually quiet, suddenly broke into a wide smile.

'I think I have it,' he said, reaching for the pile of DVDs.

'This,' he said, holding up a DVD, 'is what we should watch.'

'*Inception*?' blurted Shah.

Two and a half hours later, as the closing credits rolled, Swamy crossed his arms and leaned back in his seat with a satisfied smile.

'So what do you think? Brilliant, no?'

Modi and Shah stared back blankly with their mouths slightly open.

Swamy's smile faded. 'Did you at least get the basic idea?'

'There were no subtitles!' protested Shah.

Swamy slapped his forehead.

The next morning, Swamy began with a crash course on inception for his two colleagues. Reprising his days as a Harvard professor, Swamy laid out the elements of his plan in a lucid and engrossing lecture, using diagrams, charts and equations to supplement his ideas. Modi and Shah listened in rapt attention and furiously took notes.

'We cannot hurt the aliens,' said Swamy, pacing the room. 'We cannot even scratch their skin. The shield around their bodies makes sure of that. While I like Amit bhai's idea of deploying Somnath Bharti to spam the alien systems and bring down their shields like in *Independence Day*, we have no idea where the shield controllers are. So, until we figure out how to get the shields down, our only option is to convince them to leave of their own will. We have to make the alien commander *want* to leave earth and go back to his planet.'

He stopped near the whiteboard and read out the sentence on it, punctuating each word with a tap of his pointer. 'I will return to my planet because my prince is dead.'

'This is the idea I propose we plant in ET's subconscious. Now this is obviously an idea that ET in his conscious state will choose to reject. That is why we have to enter a shared dream state with him and plant this idea deep in his subconscious. For the idea to take root and grow in his mind, we have to go deep enough.'

Modi cleared his throat.

'You mean a dream within a dream? Two levels?'

'Three levels,' said Swamy. 'Now, if you paid any attention to the movie at all, one hour in the real world is equivalent to twenty hours in the first-level dream. This further compounds as we go deeper into the second and third levels . . .'

Someone coughed.

'Yes?' said Swamy, turning towards Modi.

Modi shrugged. 'Wasn't me.'

'Wasn't me either,' said Shah.

Swamy frowned. Shah placed a finger on his lips and flicked his eyes towards the door.

The three men tiptoed to the door and flung it open in a sudden movement. In tumbled a short moustached man in a frayed old sweater and a cheap pair of trousers.

'Shri 420!?' exclaimed Swamy incredulously.

'AK49!?' exclaimed Modi at the same time.

Kejriwal picked himself up and adjusted his muffler and AAP cap.

'Modiji, I am like your child. I look up to you to guide me,' he said with a toothy smile.

'What do you want, AK49?'

'Well, I figured that the people of this country have elected us both to serve them—you in 2014, and me in the

Delhi Assembly elections where BJP could manage only three seats. So it is our responsibility to work together.'

'So?'

'So I have come to join your team. It is what the people of Delhi want!'

'No way.'

Swamy cleared his throat. 'Modiji, if I may,' he said, and pulled Modi aside.

'Now that Shri 420 knows what we are up to, don't you think it is better to have him close where we can keep an eye on him rather than risk him sabotaging us with his nuisance?' he whispered.

Modi thought for a moment before agreeing, 'You're right, Swamyji.'

The duo turned to Kejriwal.

'All right, but no lip out of you or you are out,' said Modi.

Kejriwal brightened. 'You will not regret this, Modiji. *Yeh Kejriwal iss desh ke liye jaan bhi de sakta hai!*'

With a wary glance at the beaming Kejriwal, Swamy resumed the session.

'This is a dream-sharing device developed by the Americans,' he said, setting an open briefcase on the table in front of the team. 'Observe the timer, the wires and the machinery. As many as ten people can hook up to this device and share lucid dreams for a pre-decided duration of time controlled by this timer.'

'However,' he added, stepping back, 'the device runs on a drug called somnacin. And therein lies our first challenge. The Americans maintain strict control over their somnacin stocks. Unless we can get hold of some, we cannot undertake this operation.'

'That's hardly an issue,' said Modi cockily.

He flicked his left wrist and out slipped an iPhone from his sleeve into his palm.

'Siriben, call my BFF,' he ordered.

'Calling BFF,' replied Siri and, a moment later, the President of the United States was on the line. Modi placed the call on loudspeaker and flashed a proud smile.

'Hello, Barack! Wassup, bro!'

There was a moment's silence.

'New phone, who dis?'

Kejriwal sniggered. Modi looked momentarily stumped, but quickly recovered.

'It's Narendra!'

'Um . . . Narendra . . . ?'

'Modi! The prime minister of India! Your 4 a.m. pal!'

'Ohh! Hi Modiji. How are things?'

'Great, great. Listen, Barack, I need your help very urgently. I . . .'

'Hey Modiji, listen, I'm in the middle of something right now. Can I call you back?'

'No, no, this is important! We . . .' But the call had already disconnected.

Modi stared at his phone in disbelief. Shah and Swamy exchanged a worried glance. Kejriwal bit down on his muffler to keep a straight face.

Modi sighed deeply. 'Okay, somnacin is going to be a challenge.'

The men slouched in their seats, sullenly staring at the floor.

'I wish someone had figured out a desi workaround for this,' said Shah after several minutes of silence.

Modi brightened and sat up straight.

'You know what,' he said with a slowly spreading grin, 'I happen to know someone who might have done just that.'

A rickety autorickshaw stopped outside a ramshackle apartment in a seedy lane in Bangalore and two Sikh men in bright-coloured turbans disembarked from it. Once the autorickshaw turned the corner, one of them knocked on the rotting door. A moment later, the housekeeper came to the door and creaked it open an inch. After a brief exchange with the visitors, he opened the door wider and let the two men in.

Once inside, the housekeeper turned to the two men and folded his hands respectfully.

'Welcome, Modiji, welcome Swamyji. I am Bangarappa. I look after this place,' he said, as Modi and Swamy removed their turbans and detached their beards.

'We have come to meet Gowda,' said Swamy.

Bangarappa smiled. 'I will take you to him. Please follow me.'

The housekeeper led the two visitors through a serpentine corridor that twisted and turned a dozen times, and ended in a staircase leading downwards. Cautiously, the three men descended the steps until they reached a thick door in the basement. Bangarappa pushed it open.

A dozen men clad in white shirts and white dhotis lay sleeping on couches that seemed to be arranged like the spokes of a wheel, all pointing to the centre, where, snoring gloriously on a king-sized bed, lay Deve Gowda.

'Ten . . . twelve Karnataka MLAs . . . all connected to Gowda. My God!' said Swamy, tracing the wires going back and forth between the sleepers.

'They come here every day to share brainwaves with Gowda,' said Bangarappa. 'They sleep and dream up to four hours at a time. Twice as effective as using somnacin.'

He slapped the sleeping legislator lying on the bed next to him. The man did not even flinch.

'See? Very stable.'

Modi looked around the room, a frown on his face.

'Why do they do it?'

'Because the Assembly is off session,' smiled the housekeeper. 'After sleeping in the House all these years, this is the only way these MLAs can sleep peacefully any more.'

One of the MLAs smiled creepily in his sleep and groped at the air with his fingers.

'It is also the only way they can watch naughty stuff any more.'

Modi and Swamy paced the room, watching and examining the dreamers. Ten minutes later, they glanced at each other and shared a nod.

'We need to talk to Gowda,' Swamy told Bangarappa.

An hour later, a woozy Deve Gowda sat opposite Modi and Swamy, with a cup of extra-strong filter coffee. Gowda downed his drink in one smooth motion, returned the cup to the table and turned to his two guests.

'So what can I do for you?' asked Gowda, eyes half open.

Swamy leaned forward. 'Modiji, I and a couple of others are planning a top secret operation that will convince the alien commander to leave this planet and return home. The idea behind this operation is inception, an ingenious mechanism by which we will enter a shared dream state with the alien commander and . . . Gowdre? Gowdre?'

Gowda was fast asleep.

'Why don't you make your brief a bit shorter?' suggested Bangarappa. 'Ready?' he asked, holding an ultrasound emitting device against Gowda's ear and a finger over its switch.

'Go!'

Swamy was off the blocks like an athlete. 'We are leading a team that is planning a daring operation inspired from the movie *Inception*. As part of this operation, we will enter the alien commander's dreams and plant the idea in . . . Gowdre? Gowdre!'

'Shorter,' urged Bangarappa.

This time, Swamy took a minute to prepare himself. He sat up straight, fixed his gaze on a spot on the table and summoned all his powers of concentration. When he was ready, Bangarappa raised the ultrasound emitter.

'Three . . . two . . . one . . . Go!'

Swamy took off like a bullet from a gun.

'We are gonna plant an idea in the alien commander's mind that will make him leave earth. Will you be part of our team?'

'Yes!' exulted Swamy, overjoyed at having successfully rattled off the mission plan, until he looked up at Gowda. The former prime minister was dozing with his mouth open.

Utterly exasperated, he turned to Bangarappa. The housekeeper offered a reassuring nod and said, 'Don't worry. I'll arrange for him to join you in Delhi.'

Bangarappa kept his promise. The next day, Deve Gowda was snoozing in Swamy's pad instead of his apartment in

Bengaluru. Kejriwal, the engineer in the team, tinkered with the dream-sharing device to make it work with Deve Gowda instead of somnacin.

Swamy, meanwhile, resumed his lesson.

'The next challenge is to figure out how to go about planting the idea in his mind,' he said, tapping the pointer against his palm as he paced the room.

'This is what I propose,' he said, turning to face his audience. 'In the first-level dream, one of us will disguise himself as an old woman and suggest to ET that she found the prince when his shuttle crash-landed here all those years back. Obviously no one knows if it actually did, but ET seems to be sure, so he will most likely believe her, especially if the acting is convincing.'

'Hmm,' said Modi, 'I can do that. I can play the old woman convincingly.'

'Great,' said Swamy. 'Then when we go one level deeper, ET will seek the old woman to find out more. We will meet ET in the second-level dream and help him find the old woman, which he will because she would be a projection in ET's mind. We will then convince ET to enter a shared dream state with us and the old woman in order to find the secrets she is hiding. But we would really be breaking deep into his subconscious where we will plant the idea that his prince is dead.'

'Uh,' said Modi, scratching his beard, 'this went slightly over the head, Swamyji, but I think we get the basic idea.'

'Yeah?' asked Swamy doubtfully, glancing at a vacuous-looking Shah.

'Yeah. Besides, you will be there to lead it.'

'Hmm. Okay. Now,' Swamy said as he began to pace again, 'like in the movie, down there in the dreams, we may face resistance from hostile projections. We need to avoid, outrun and maybe even fight these projections. It might be a good idea to rope in another member to our team to add some firepower.'

'Do you have anyone in mind?'

Swamy smiled. 'Actually, yes. I think I know just the guy for this.'

Suddenly, Kejriwal flung a screwdriver across the room and threw up his hands.

'Modiji is not letting me work by distracting me with his non-stop talking,' he exclaimed. *'Please, Modiji, mujhe kaam karne dijiye! Mein achha kaam karta hoon!'*

Modi glared at Kejriwal, before turning to Swamy, 'Let's go get your guy.'

A thousand miles away, in a posh Mumbai suburb, the champion of the nation, Arnab Goswami, stepped out of the master bedroom of his elegantly furnished apartment and sneaked into his four-year-old son's bedroom.

Ever since the aliens attacked Times Now's office in Lower Parel, he had had little to do. He stayed confined to his apartment, watching in frustration as day after day politicians went unquestioned, issues to be outraged over went untouched and Pakistani spokespersons went unassailed. The aliens clearly knew what they were doing. By putting him out of action, they had struck a devastating blow to the nation's psyche.

Scratching his week-old stubble, Arnab threw a quick glance at the sleeping form of his son followed by a furtive peek at the door, then tiptoed to a small table in the corner and squatted in front of it. He grabbed the Milton water bottle lying by the side and spilled some water in the middle of the table. Then, slowly, he opened the table drawer and pulled out a stuffed tiger and a stuffed elephant. He placed the elephant near the puddle of water and the tiger at the edge of the table behind the elephant.

'The elephant is quietly drinking water in the forest,' he whispered and dunked the elephant's trunk in the puddle. 'Drink, elephant, drink!'

'A hungry tiger spots the elephant and decides to make a meal of him,' he continued in a whisper and slowly moved the tiger towards the elephant. 'Grrr . . .'

'The tiger leaps at the elephant!' he exclaimed and dashed the two toys together. 'He goes for the neck, but the elephant is too strong. His trunk whacks the tiger away. The tiger jumps again and the two animals thrash around in a violent scuffle. Eventually, injured and insulted, the tiger gives up the idea and slips away.'

After having the two toys scuffle for a few moments, Arnab wiped the table clean and set the two toys side by side facing him. He reached into the drawer and pulled out two more toys, a stuffed crocodile and a stuffed lion. Then he cupped his mouth and began vocalizing a soundtrack rather like the opening tune of the *Newshour*.

'Good evening, ladies and gentlemen. Welcome to the *Newshour* debate. In a shocking incident today, an elephant brazenly attacked an animal that is placed above it in the food chain. What is the animal kingdom in this nation coming to, ladies and gentlemen? Is this the world our forefathers dreamt of when they gave us the Constitution? On the *Newshour* tonight, your channel will ask tough questions of the animals involved!'

'Joining us in the debate are Mr Tiger, Mr Elephant, Mr Crocodile and the king of the jungle, Mr Lion. Welcome, gentlemen. We will start with a direct question to Mr Elephant. Mr Elephant, what possible justification do you have for this cowardly act?'

Arnab grabbed the trunk of the stuffed elephant and tugged it up and down. 'Well, Arnab, you see . . .' he said in a squeaky made-up voice that elephants supposedly used in Arnab's world.

'Why did you attack the tiger, Mr Elephant?' he demanded in his own voice, interrupting himself.

'It was Mr Tiger who attacked me first!' the elephant said.

'Let's bring Mr Tiger into the debate. Mr Tiger, I have the highest regard for you. But if you will allow me to ask, why did you attack Mr Elephant?'

Arnab picked up the tiger with his other hand and began shaking its head to and fro. Assuming a gruff voice, he said, 'Arnab, I am a tiger, I am a carnivore. If I cannot kill and eat animals like Mr Elephant, what will I eat? I cannot eat grass! What I did was within the laws of nature!'

'You hit the nail on the head, Mr Tiger. How do you respond to this, Mr Elephant? Are you now willing to apologize to Mr Tiger in front of the nation?' Arnab demanded, turning to the elephant.

'Arnab, I . . . but . . . I mean . . . don't I have the right to survive?' squeaked the elephant.

'You are tying yourself up in knots today, Mr Elephant,' declared Arnab. 'Let's open up the debate, ladies and gentlemen. Let me bring in Mr Lion. Mr Lion, what in God's name is happening in your forest?'

Assuming a deep baritone, Arnab mimed a reply for the lion. 'First of all, I would like to express my sympathies with Mr Tiger and Mr Elephant for suffering injuries. Having said that, I cannot be held responsible for . . .'

'The buck stops with you, Mr Lion!' thundered Arnab. 'Tigers and elephants are butchering each other in broad daylight! Are animals safe any more in your forest, Mr Lion?'

'Allow me to complete, Arnab. You cannot blame me . . .'

'You are just digging a grave for yourself, Mr Lion!' declared Arnab, interrupting himself yet again.

'Arnab, you very well know that our forest is a federal system. Law and order is a state subject. So you should be putting this question to Mr Crocodile who oversees the area around the lake.'

'Yes, I will, Mr Lion. Mr Crocodile, you were at the scene, you saw the whole thing. What did you . . .'

'ARE YOU PLAYING WITH BUNTY'S TOYS AGAIN?'

Arnab froze mid-sentence. The blood drained from his face. He let go of the stuffed crocodile and slowly turned around with a hangdog expression to face the woman bearing down on him with apoplectic rage.

Mrs Goswami glowered at her husband for an entire minute. Arnab wilted under her gaze and instinctively curled himself into a ball. Bunty, who had been up for a while and was following the debate with significant interest, looked mildly disappointed at the interruption.

Exasperation replaced anger on Mrs Goswami's face. Turning skywards, she wailed, 'Why, dear Lord, why did those damned aliens take down his office? I just can't take any more of this! Isn't there a job he can go to, so that I can live in peace?'

'Yes, there is,' said a voice from the door. The Goswamis spun towards the source in unison.

Subramanian Swamy walked up to Arnab and put both hands on his shoulders.

'The nation needs you, Arnab. Will you come?'

Tears welled up in Arnab's eyes. With a quivering lip, he looked up at Swamy.

'Yes!'

'What do we do once we plant the idea?' asked Modi.

The team, now numbering six, was back at Swamy's pad. They sat around a table, amidst pens, notepads and half-filled cups of tea. Deve Gowda lay slumbering with his head back against the top rail of his chair.

'How does one wake up if there is still time left on the clock?'

'Oh, I know! We bump him off,' exclaimed Shah. 'I got that part in the movie.'

'No. With this level of sedation,' said Swamy, gesturing at the snoring Gowda, 'if we die in the dream, we will go into limbo.'

'What's that?' asked Kejriwal.

'It's an unconstructed dream space that has nothing but raw infinite subconscious. We could get stuck there for a long time.'

'So how do we wake up after the job is done?' Modi persisted.

'Using a kick,' replied Swamy.

'What is a kick? The nation demands to know,' said Arnab.

Swamy flashed a superlative smile.

'This, my ignoramus friend, is a kick,' he said and, with a casual movement, lifted Gowda's chair by one of its front legs, throwing it off balance. The chair toppled backwards with a thud and would have woken any other man on the planet sitting on it. Gowda, however, stayed stuck to the fallen chair and continued to snore.

Swamy looked flummoxed.

'Er, perhaps it is better explained in words,' he said after a moment. 'A kick is a feeling of falling that jolts you awake from a dream. At each level, one member of the team will be left behind to set up the kick for the others to wake up.'

'Now, the important thing is to synchronize this kick across the three levels. The usual technique to do this is to play a musical number—we tend to hear sounds even in a dream—so when the music comes on, we can set up the kick and wake up.'

'What music will we be using?' asked Kejriwal.

'Vande Mataram, of course!' said Modi.

Kejriwal jumped to his feet.

'I object to this,' he exclaimed. 'I will not let this operation be hijacked by communal elements.'

Modi shut his eyes and rubbed his forehead, trying to calm himself.

'*Mein aapko bata doon, Modiji!*' continued Kejriwal. '*Aap se nahi darne waala yeh Kejriwal. Mein aakhri saans tak ladta rahunga iss desh ke liye!*'

Modi had had enough. He leapt to his feet and began reeling off his idea of India at the top of his voice, 'Idea of

India, *Satyamev Jayate*, Idea of India, *Ahimsa Parmo Dharma*, Idea of India . . .' which only made Kejriwal shout louder. Back and forth they went, *'Aapko pata nahi mein kis mitti ka bana hoon . . .'*, 'Idea of India, *Vasudhaiva Kutumbakam . . .'*, *'Aapke CBI, aur tut-panjiyon se, aur geedad-bhabkiyon se nahi darne waala . . .'*, 'Idea of India, *Ekam Sad Viprah Bahudha Vadanti . . .'*

Unable to restrain himself, Arnab too waded into the melee. 'Just a minute, gentlemen!' he cried, shouting over Modi and Kejriwal. 'Let me moderate this debate. One at a time, gentlemen. Let him speak, Mr Modi, let him . . .'

'SHUT UP!' hollered Swamy.

Instantly the room went silent.

Swamy took a deep breath.

'Now, Shri 420, what music do you want to use?'

'My rendition of *Insaan ka insaan se ho bhaichara*. I sang it when I first took oath as Delhi's CM. It is a secular song that applies to all of humanity,' said Kejriwal, and began to loudly sing the 1959 classic.

By the time he was done, the rest of them had retreated to the farthest corners of the room and were curled in a foetal position with their hands pressed over their ears.

'What the hell was that?' gasped a startled Gowda, wide awake for the first time that week.

Swamy gawked at the conscious Gowda. 'Wow!' he said. 'That settles it then. We will use Shri 420's song to synchronize the kick.'

The men nodded in agreement.

'Well, gentlemen, that brings our preparatory phase to an end.'

There was a brief silence, during which it dawned on the men that the time for talk was over. It was time for action.

Slowly, the team members converged in a circle in the middle of the room. For a moment, they stood regarding each other with blazing eyes. Then, Modi thrust his hand forward. One by one the greatest political warriors of India joined their hands to the pile, until only Kejriwal was left.

'*Sab mile huey hai ji,*' he muttered and added his hand to the heap.

And then, boisterous whoops, catcalls and chants of '*Bharat mata ki jai*' rent the room and reverberated in the air over and over again for several minutes.

When the room finally calmed down, Amit Shah suddenly froze.

'Wait,' he said, 'there's still one problem.'

'What's that?' asked Swamy.

'If we cannot put even a scratch on the alien commander, how will we get him to sleep? We cannot use tranquilizers. We cannot use chemicals. We cannot conk him on his head. Hell, the aliens don't even sleep! How are we going to get him to dream?'

Swamy and Modi exchanged a knowing smile.

TEN

Modi's Dream

THE NEXT DAY, at the break of dawn, a diminutive old man in a faded blue turban slowly and stiffly made his way towards the thick door of the sprawling 7, RCR bungalow allotted to the democratically elected prime minister of India, which was now occupied by the alien leader who had supplanted him. Behind him, strewn here and there on the garden path leading to the door, were the still forms of alien soldiers tasked with guarding their commander.

As Modi and the others watched from beyond the fence of the compound, another guard accosted the turbaned man just outside the door. The elderly man made no sudden movements. From their vantage point, they saw him slowly rotate towards the guard and look up at him. Seconds later, the soldier went down like a sack of potatoes and remained still.

'Damn,' whispered Shah in evident awe.

The turbaned man rigidly swivelled back towards the door and rang the doorbell.

It was the alien commander himself who answered the door, wearing a T-shirt that said 'I am PM, bitch'.

'Yes?'

Dr Manmohan Singh stared back at Qaal-za with unblinking eyes.

The alien commander frowned. Then his eyes widened as he spotted the inert forms of his guards behind Dr Singh.

'What the . . .' he sputtered, stumbling backwards.

Dr Singh stepped in and launched into his thousandth speech on the state of the Indian economy.

'The Indian economy has grown at an average of 8 per cent per annum over the last decade. Recently, our growth rate declined to 5 per cent because of recession in the global economy. The rupee has depreciated sharply as well, partly because of the prospect of the Federal Reserve tapering its policy of quantitative easing that has led to the reversal of capital flows, causing general weakness in emerging market currencies. However, the fundamentals of the Indian economy continue to remain strong. I see growth bottoming out in the near future . . .'

In the span of a minute, the alien commander's face played host to a dramatic medley of emotions. First there was confusion as his mind attempted to process what was happening. Confusion gave way to panic as his mind began to comprehend the assault and the extent of it. Then as wave upon wave of robotically delivered, mind-numbing economic jargon inundated his senses, his eyes began to glaze over and his mind began to lose its grip on reality.

'. . . Our medium-term objective is to reduce the current account deficit. Our short-term objective is to finance the current account deficit in an orderly fashion. We will make every effort to maintain a macro economic framework friendly to foreign capital inflows to enable orderly financing of the current account deficit. Reforms are the need of the hour . . .'

The weight of mountains was on the alien commander's eyelids. He swayed unsteadily, arms flailing for support, as lights began to go off one by one in his mind. A small part of his consciousness that was getting smaller by the second was still fighting to stay awake for some incomprehensible reason.

'. . . There are many reforms that require political consensus. But if we all work hard we can attain 8 per cent growth . . .'

The alien commander crashed to the ground like a bag of bones.

Ten minutes later, when Modi and his team sneaked into the living room, they found Dr Singh sitting calmly on a chair, staring at a spot on the wall straight ahead, and the alien commander curled into a foetal position at his feet, snoring loudly.

Amit Shah nudged the slumbering alien with a toe and whistled.

'Deadly stuff, this is.'

'Lethal,' agreed Swamy. 'In fact, I'm surprised he held on for so long. I've never made it past the "growth bottoming out" line.'

'Great job, *paaji*,' said Modi.

'The nation is impressed,' added Arnab.

'Theek hai,' deadpanned Dr Singh.

Deve Gowda stifled a yawn.

'Let's get to work, guys. This is the longest I've been up so far.'

Swiftly but silently, the team set the scene for the operation. Arnab and Kejriwal hauled the alien commander into the master bedroom. Modi and Shah pulled in a couch, a couple of reclining chairs and a spare mattress, while Swamy set up the dream-sharing device on the bedside table. Gowda found a felt pen, scrawled 'Do not disturb' on a large piece of paper and stuck it to the outside of the door. He then sat Dr Manmohan Singh on a chair in the corridor, shut the door and turned the key. The six men made themselves comfortable on the various pieces of furniture.

'Remember,' said Swamy, just as they were about to go under, 'we will be in Modiji's dream at the first level. We have exactly three hours before Qaal-za wakes up. Good luck. May Bharat mata give us the strength to defeat left-liberal alien forces. Vande Mataram!'

'Vande Mataram!' chimed everyone except Kejriwal.

Swamy pushed the button on the dream-sharing device.

'*Sab mile huey hai ji,*' muttered Kejriwal as the world around him began to blur.

The scent of the river stirred him out of his reverie. Kejriwal opened his eyes and the world slowly came into focus.

A turquoise-blue river rushed and foamed a few metres from him, splashing a chilly spray as it dashed against the concrete riverbank. In the distance, a quaint-looking boat packed with people bobbed on the sparkling water. Across the river, a string of skyscrapers rose sharply into the sky, spotless glass windows glimmering in the sunlight. As he watched, a helicopter descended on to the roof of one of the buildings.

Behind him, on the riverfront, a number of people milled about, talking, laughing and clicking pictures. Men, women and children of all kinds—Caucasians, Africans, East Asians and Middle-Easterners—relaxed, frolicked or meandered in the stunningly landscaped gardens and the elegantly designed strolling area. Everything was strikingly beautiful and spotlessly clean. Despite himself, Kejriwal felt his pulse slow down and a sense of peace seep into his consciousness.

Then he saw Modi, Swamy and Shah marching towards him in the distance, and his pulse shot right back up.

'What is this place, Modiji? Are we in some foreign country? Even in your dream, you cannot help but fly abroad, can you?' he scowled when the trio reached him. 'How are we supposed to get to Delhi? This mission is already a failure and you are solely responsible for it, Modiji!'

'Don't get your muffler in a twist,' scoffed Modi, striding past Kejriwal. 'We are in Ahmedabad. Let's find the others. Come on!'

The four men quickly set about finding the rest of the team. Arnab was easiest to locate. The journalist was in the middle of a commotion down the shore, loudly arguing with a Pakistani tourist.

'Yours is not a legitimate nation, Mister Pakistani Tourist!' he screamed, as Shah dragged him away.

Deve Gowda took a little more searching but was soon discovered snoring on a bench in a quiet corner of the park. Swamy slapped him awake. Then, led by a brisk Modi, the team strode out of the riverfront area and turned into a busy street.

The mood on the street was drastically different from the relaxed ambience of the riverfront. Skyscrapers loomed on either side, draping the street in their shadows. Men and women in business suits briskly strode all around them. There wasn't anyone on the street who wasn't dressed in business formals. Even the street vendors wore suits as they hawked their wares.

'Apples! Have some apples! Apple stands for A Pure, Pleasing, Luscious Eatable! Or take these oranges! They will make for Outstandingly Ripe, Appetizing, Nutritious, Globular, Evening Snacks,' cried one such suited vendor on the pavement.

A woman striding past his cart paused mid-stride, scanned the goods and smiled, 'Okay, I'll take two kilos of apples.'

The vendor made the sale and followed it up with a selfie with the satisfied customer.

As the group marched further down the road, the buildings got taller and the cars fancier. The world's biggest names seemed to have their offices on the street. Apple, Google, Microsoft, Boeing, AT&T, Airbus, Bank of America, Citigroup, Coca-Cola, Walt Disney—they were all there. One by one, Modi pointed them out to the awestruck group.

'Make in India,' he beamed.

Gigantic electronic billboards layered the walls of buildings and compound walls, flashing HD-quality advertisements. Iris scanners installed on these electronic screens flickered continuously, reading and identifying pedestrians in the vicinity and customizing ads in real time. One such billboard addressed them in a woman's throaty voice as they walked past.

'Having trouble keeping track of all your cases, Swamyji? Use our Personal Organizer software and track cases, raids, ED notices on TDK, PC, BC, Buddhu and many more!'

'Vande Mataram, Amit bhai! Visit our page on Amazon for our latest range of cutting-edge wide-lens spy cameras. Saheb will be impressed!'

'Hello there, AK49. Running out of vessels to hold all your raita? Check out the new Milton range of stainless steel utensils!'

'Digital India,' chirped Modi, grinning at the scowling Kejriwal.

Presently they arrived at an intersection, where Modi signalled to the rest of the group to stop. A massive digital countdown timer installed over the signal counted down to zero as they waited on the sidewalk watching the 1000-odd men and women briskly go about their business.

Amit Shah sighed. 'We will never find Qaal-za in this crowd.'

The digital timer hit zero and a loud gong went off. Instantly, everyone and everything on the intersection froze. Cars came to a standstill. Pedestrians stopped in their tracks. Even the breeze seemed to have died for a moment.

The next second, stillness gave way to chaos. Pedestrians, drivers and passengers suddenly began to run hither-thither in a mad scramble. Ten seconds later, much to the amazement of the men watching from the sidewalk, the people on the intersection arranged themselves into a giant grid formation. Somewhere, an Om chant began, loud and resonant, and the thousand men and women in business suits began performing *suryanamaskar* in perfect synchrony.

'Yoga hour,' said Modi, grinning at his stupefied fellow dreamers. 'Amit bhai, check who's not in formation.'

Shah pulled out a pair of binoculars and scanned the scene.

'There!' he exclaimed, pointing to a confused-looking figure in the distance that seemed out of sync with the rest of the yoga practitioners. The team sprinted towards him, and sure enough, it was Qaal-za. Swamy sneaked up behind him and smothered him with a chloroform-laden towel. Bereft of his shield in Modi's dream, the alien commander went out like a light.

Qaal-za came to with a groan. Blearily, he opened his eyes and found himself in a small dark room. A withered old woman sat across the table, watching him with a dispassionate expression. He tried to get up, only to realize he was bound to the chair. He opened his mouth to say something, only to find he was gagged as well.

The old woman wordlessly watched the alien commander as he grappled uselessly against the ropes that bound him. When Qaal-za eventually gave up his struggle and sagged with a resigned expression, the old woman began speaking.

'Give up the search for your prince,' she said in a tremulous voice. 'Nothing will come out of it. Go back to your planet.'

'Whomm . . . armmm . . . yoummm?' stuttered Qaal-za through the gag.

With a trembling hand, the old woman placed a red pendant on the table. Qaal-za's eyes grew as wide as saucers.

'I am the one who found and raised him,' she said quietly.

Overwhelmed with emotion, Qaal-za found a sudden burst of energy in his arms and snapped the ropes that bound him. He leapt to his feet and shoved aside the table between him and the old woman, when suddenly, a hand clamped his mouth from behind and a sweet smell overwhelmed his senses. The room and the old woman began to blur, the world tilted and the ground rushed up to meet him, before everything faded to black.

'Do you think he bought it?' asked Modi, pulling the old woman's mask off his face.

'I think so,' said Shah, looking down at the unconscious form of Qaal-za. 'It was fairly believable anyway. It's not like we promised to deposit Rs 15 lakh in his bank account.'

Kejriwal sniggered. Modi glared at Shah, immediately drawing out a sheepish expression.

'I am sure he bought it,' said Swamy. 'Now when we take him one level deeper, he will look for the old woman to find out what she knows. He will find his projection of her, who will obviously not know anything, because she is his projection of her and would only know what he knows, which is nothing. We will then help him break into her mind, but in reality, we will be breaking into *his* mind to plant our idea.'

The others stared at Swamy with glazed expressions.

'Never mind,' sighed Swamy, 'let's just find a safe place where we can go to sleep and enter the second level.'

With Arnab and Gowda carrying the unconscious Qaal-za, the group crept out of the room and stepped into the street.

Something shiny flashed past Modi, just inches from his ear. Modi spun around reflexively and found a Sahitya

Akademi trophy sticking out from a crevice in the wall behind them.

'What the . . .'

Across the street, from within a dark alley, stepped out the harbinger of the award *wapsi* movement.

'Nayantara Sahgal?' blurted Modi.

Three more Sahitya Akademi trophies came hurtling towards them from the shadows behind Sahgal. This time, the projectiles found their mark. The sharp ends of the trophies buried themselves into Swamy's arm, Arnab's shoulder and Kejriwal's groin.

'Mummy!' cried Kejriwal.

'Amma!' cried Swamy.

'NATION!' cried Arnab.

Panic-stricken, the group broke into a run. Across the street, Sahgal issued a rallying cry. Liberals began to pour into the street from alleys, bylanes, nooks and crannies, like hordes of Agent Smith clones in the *Matrix* movies.

'What is happening?' yelled Modi as he tore down the street.

'We are being attacked by the projections of the dreamer, which in this case is you,' Swamy shouted back. 'If they catch us and kill us, we will end up in limbo and the mission will fail.'

Behind Sahgal, thirty more Sahitya Akademi-winners jumped out of the shadows and started hurling their awards at the fleeing dreamers. A few blocks up the street, historian Ramachandra Guha leapt from the veranda of a 300-year-old colonial building and joined the chase, followed by Irfan Habib and forty other historians. Fifty metres behind Modi, a hundred scientists and academics joined the chase, led by a wild-eyed P.M. Bhargava wielding his Padma Bhushan like a morning star. Army veterans from the OROP agitation sprinted along the roofs of the buildings on either side of the street, hurling their medals at the group like shuriken. A hundred metres ahead, another large group comprising film-makers led by Dibakar Banerjee, mediapersons led by Rajdeep Sardesai, armchair liberals led by Shobhaa De and other assorted Modi-haters led by Arundhati Roy swarmed out and blocked the street. Amidst all this, Aamir Khan and Kiran Rao ran along the road divider with their arms flailing, screaming, 'It's not safe! Leave this country! Worry for your children! Leave this country!'

'We are trapped!' exclaimed Shah.

'No, we aren't. Follow me, mitron!' said Modi, and disappeared down an entrance to a metro subway.

With the liberal horde close on their heels, the six men, carrying the unconscious alien between them, sprinted down the stairs and raced across a sprawling ticketing lobby. Led by Modi, they leapt over the turnstiles and sprinted down another flight of stairs that led to a sparkling platform, where a swanky bullet train stood waiting.

'Ahmedabad to Delhi in two hours!' exclaimed Modi triumphantly, ducking just out of reach of a couple of Padma Shris.

Just as the first few members of the liberal horde jumped on to the platform behind them, the bullet train sounded its horn and began moving.

'Come on, mitron!' shouted Modi as he grasped the handrail outside the door to a rail coach and hauled himself in. Behind him, Arnab and Gowda threw the unconscious form of Qaal-za in, and climbed in one after the other. Shah and Swamy, their faces red, were next, barely making it into the rapidly accelerating train. By the time it was Kejriwal's turn to jump in, the train was moving fast.

Kejriwal bit down hard on his muffler and ran as fast as he could. The handrail, however, remained just out of reach. Grunting, he reached within for one last burst of acceleration, but the train accelerated that much more. Inch by inch, the handrail began to pull away, and his heart began to sink. Just as he decided to give up and surrender to the fanatical projections snapping at his heels, a hand stretched out from the door, grabbed his hand *DDLJ* style, and swung him in.

Relieved beyond measure, Kejriwal looked up to thank his rescuer and found a beaming Modi looking down at him. The half-smile froze on Kejriwal's face. For a few seconds, he groped for words, before his mouth twisted into the familiar scowl.

'Where are the police while fanatical projections attack the aam aadmi? Have they been directed by their master Modi not to do anything?' he demanded.

Modi slapped his palm against his forehead and stormed off.

Outside, just as the last few coaches of the train pulled out of the platform, a hundred projections climbed in and started making their way towards the engine.

Swamy retrieved the dream-sharing device from an overhead bin and began setting it up in the middle of the coach, while Shah and Arnab went about locking every entry and exit in their coach and the three coaches trailing theirs, to put as many obstacles as possible between them and the projections.

'We probably have an hour before the projections break in, which should give us enough time down below,' said

Swamy as he spread out the wires. 'Amit bhai will hold the fort while we go in.'

With that, Modi, Swamy, Arnab, Gowda and the unconscious Qaal-za pushed back their seats and settled in to enter the next dream level.

'Remember,' said Swamy, as he closed his eyes, 'this is 420's dream.'

'No,' said Kejriwal dreamily as he drifted off. *'Yeh desh ki janta ka dream hai . . .'*

ELEVEN

Desh ki Janta ka Dream

Modiji hai hai!
Modiji hai hai!

AN OVERPOWERING STINK of sweat greeted Modi as he opened his eyes. He found himself amidst a raucous crowd of broom-wielding folks jumping up and down in a mad frenzy, shouting slogans at the top of their voices.

Akkad bakkad bambe bo!
Modiji, Kejriwal ko kaam karne do!

The neighbourhood seemed vaguely familiar. Modi stood on his toes to get a glimpse of the surroundings. Between flailing hands and swishing brooms, he made out the outline of a large Lutyens bungalow. Realization hit him a moment later; they were gathered outside his residence in 7, RCR.

Roses are red, violets are blue!
How to govern, Modiji has no clue!

Modi wrapped a scarf around the lower half of his face to avoid recognition. Someone thrust a broom in his hand. Modi raised it high and pretended to join in on the slogan-shouting.

Modiji humein mat sikhao!
Pehle apni degree dikhao!

The sloganeering carried on for several minutes, until a siren went off somewhere. A recorded message in Kejriwal's voice sounded from a nearby loudspeaker.

'Thank you, *doston*, that's the end of dharna hour today! See you again tomorrow, same time same place. May the Almighty protect you all from Modiji.'

With one last lusty cheer, the crowd began to disperse. Keeping his head low, Modi swiftly walked away from the scene.

Ten minutes later, when he was by himself, he began to look around. The area looked nothing like the Lutyens Zone he knew. Gone were the elegant bungalows and manicured lawns. Instead, a squalid slum stretched on either side of the street as far as the eye could see. A makeshift hut sat smack in the middle of the pedestrian walkway. A board with the words 'Just regularized!' hung across its front door.

The road was bustling with traffic. The majority of the vehicles were autorickshaws and two-wheelers. AAP volunteers threaded in and out of the traffic, directing vehicles and handing out roses to the handful of cars plying on the street.

By the roadside, large billboards were installed at intervals of 100 metres, each flashing a message from the Delhi government in big bold letters.

'Thank you for supporting mod-3 in traffic. If you have driven out in your car today, please divide your registration number by 3 and check if the remainder is 2. If it is anything else, please return home and take the metro instead!' read the first billboard.

'Delhi government is pleased to announce that along with electricity, water, Wi-Fi, medicines and groceries, now chaddi-baniyans are free as well! Inform us if your nearby shop does not give you your chaddi-baniyan free of cost, so that our volunteers can visit the owner and give him a rose,' read the second.

'Thank you for supporting odd-even in electricity and water. Because of your cooperation and the honesty of our government, electricity outages on the days power is available has gone down by 30%!' read the third.

'Delhi government will cancel the licences of chaddi-baniyan shops that refuse to supply underwear to customers free of cost,' read the fourth.

'Please Modiji, send the funds that you owe the people of Delhi. Please let the honest Delhi government do its work,' read the fifth.

'Delhi government is pleased to announce the first odd-even pilot of chaddi-baniyan next month! We expect your warm cooperation!' read the sixth.

After walking for more than twenty minutes, Modi arrived at an intersection and stopped for a breather. Just when he began to wonder if he would ever find the others, he spotted Swamy, Arnab and Gowda standing amidst a small crowd outside a roadside shop jostling to catch a glimpse of a small TV set.

'Finally found you guys,' said Modi, slapping them on their backs cheerfully. 'Where's AK49?'

In reply, Swamy pointed at the TV. A brightly lit stage with a castle in the background appeared on the screen. A familiar soundtrack rang out, drawing a cheer from the crowd gathered outside the tea shop. Firepots exploded along the front of the stage and the camera zoomed in on the castle door and on the words 'India's Got Talent—Auditions' painted on it. The door parted in the middle and in walked the judges of the day—Karan Johar, Malaika Arora and Kirron Kher—waving vigorously to the studio audience. Dancing and clapping, the three made their way to their seats at the judges' desk. Kirron Kher pretend-slapped Karan Johar on his face, who in turn pretend-slapped Malaika Arora on her arm. Then they all sat down.

'Okay, let's begin!' said Kirron Kher.

The camera cut to the empty stage, where, from the left, a short, bespectacled and moustached man in a loose-fitting shirt, dirty grey pants and an AAP cap walked over to the microphone and joined his hands in a namaste.

'Tell us about yourself, darling,' said Karan Johar.

'*Ji, mein Arvind Kejriwal hoon.* I'm an aam aadmi with no aukaat.'

'What do you do?' said Malaika Arora.

'I review movies, level allegations and govern Delhi.'

'Okay, Arvind, what is the talent you are going to show us today?' said Kirron Kher.

'You ask me any question on any issue, and I will convincingly blame it on Modi.'

Karan Johar exchanged an intrigued glance with Malaika.

'All right! Let's see it,' said Malaika. 'Let me start with something simple. Why is there so much pollution?'

'Because, in the name of so-called development, Modiji has increased coal production in the country to record levels, which has polluted our air. Unlike me, who shuns security, Modiji has so much security that the extra vehicles that go on the road every time he travels to and from the airport have increased pollution by 10 per cent. His minister Nitin Gadkari is single-handedly reducing the forest cover in the country by urinating on plants and trees and corroding their roots. He has admitted this on record. The honest government in Delhi is trying its best to compensate for Modi's actions through the odd-even or the mod-3, mod-4 and mod-5 rules, but instead of encouraging us, Modiji's online supporters troll and abuse us.'

The studio audience, filled with people sporting AAP caps, erupted in applause. After the noise died down, Karan Johar smiled mischievously. 'All right, honey, I have one. Ranbir–Katrina break-up—who is to blame? Ranbir or Katrina?'

'Neither. Modiji is to blame,' declared Kejriwal without a second's hesitation. 'It is because of the relentless attacks on minorities under Modiji's government that Katrina, daughter of a Muslim father and a Christian mother, felt scared and insecure and wanted to get married soon. Ranbir, however, wasn't ready. This caused differences between them which ultimately led to their break-up. Modiji must apologize to both their families and all young lovers in India!'

Once again, the people in the studio sprang from their seats and clapped enthusiastically, while Karan Johar sat with a hand on his mouth, wearing an exaggerated expression of horror. Outside the tea shop, Modi watched the cheering mob of onlookers in disbelief.

Kirron Kher waited for the audience to settle before speaking up. 'What about global warming?'

Pat came Kejriwal's reply. 'Modiji is to blame for global warming too. Modi-loving media will never tell you this, but the truth is, methane is thirty times more potent a greenhouse gas compared to carbon dioxide. And one of the major contributors to methane in the atmosphere is cow farts. By enforcing ban on cow slaughter across the country, Modiji has drastically increased the number of cows in the country. Which means that a lot more cows are now farting day in and day out, releasing a lot more methane to the atmosphere. This, in turn, is causing significantly more heat to be trapped, because of which global temperatures are going up.'

'Oh my God! Modiji is so bad, *yaa*,' exclaimed a wide-eyed Malaika, even as the audience roared its approval.

The show went on like this for the next few minutes with the issues and questions getting increasingly arbitrary, but Kejriwal took them all.

'What causes constipation in people?' asked a judge.

'Modiji, of course! Because of his poor water management, 70 per cent of the country is plunged in drought. People don't have drinking water to wash down their food, because of which they are getting constipated!' retorted Kejriwal.

'Why did Kattappa kill Bahubali?'

'Because he was a Modi agent and because Bahubali thought Modi's degrees were fake!'

'Why did the chicken cross the road?'

'Because Modiji isn't giving control of police to the Delhi government. Otherwise no chicken would dare to cross the road!'

After over fifteen such issues, all of which were comprehensively blamed on Modi by the Delhi CM, Kirron Kher slammed the desk in a sudden outburst of excitement.

'Okay, try linking *this* to Modiji!' she said with a confident smile. 'Who is responsible for Partition?'

'Come on, *yaa*,' Karan Johar chided Kirron Kher, 'this is not fair. Modiji wasn't even born. How can he connect . . .'

'Modiji is responsible for Partition,' Kejriwal declared without hesitation.

The judges' jaws dropped in unison.

'Modiji time-travelled to the early twentieth century and communalized the atmosphere. This made Jinnah feel insecure and unwelcome in his own country, just like Muslims in India are feeling today. This led Jinnah to espouse the two-nation theory, ultimately resulting in the partition of India.'

This time, even the AAP volunteers in the crowd gaped at Kejriwal.

'But . . . there's no such thing as a time machine!' sputtered Kirron Kher.

'That's because Modiji destroyed it after using it because he didn't want the honest AAP government to use it to go back in time and eliminate corruption.'

'What? This is unbelievable . . . this can't be true!'

'If it is not true, why isn't Modiji speaking up to deny it?' demanded Kejriwal.

The judges had no answer.

Slowly, Karan Johar rose to his feet, then Malaika, and finally Kirron Kher. Shaking their heads in admiration, they delivered a standing ovation.

'I bow down to your talent!' said Malaika. *'Meri taraf se haan!'*

'Today, I see a finalist!' exclaimed Karan Johar. *'Meri taraf se haan!'*

'Meri taraf se bhi haan!' said Kirron Kher, wiping a tear from her eye.

Outside the tea shop, the crowd celebrated with uninhibited joy, hooting, screaming and high-fiving each other. A couple of revellers broke away from the group and set fire to an effigy resembling Modi in the middle of the road. Some others started a chant of *'Paanch saal Kejriwal'* which was promptly picked up by everyone.

Avoiding the eyes of the raucous men, Modi, Swamy, Arnab and Gowda made to sneak away from the spot, when a blue WagonR with Kejriwal at the wheel and Qaal-za riding shotgun rolled to a stop in front of them.

'People did not make you PM so that you waste time watching TV by the roadside, Modiji,' jeered Kejriwal. 'Get in, and I will show you how an honest government works.'

Throwing the grinning Kejriwal a withering look, Modi and the others squeezed into the WagonR. Kejriwal threw the car into gear, executed a sharp U-turn and took off down the road.

'Uh, hello, Qaal-za bhai,' said Modi tentatively, unsure of what the alien commander remembered from reality.

'Hello Modiji,' replied Qaal-za warmly. 'Thank you for agreeing to help me extract the truth from the old woman. It means a lot to me.'

'You found the old woman?' asked Swamy, surprised.

'She is in the dickey,' said Qaal-za. 'We tried to interrogate her ourselves but she keeps passing out. We didn't know what to do. That's when Arvind suggested that we come find you.'

'I see,' said Swamy, glaring at Kejriwal. 'You will never learn the truth by shaking her up. There is only one way to find out what she's hiding.'

'What's that?'

'We need to break into her subconscious.'

'How do we do that?'

Swamy folded his arms and sat back in his seat with a smile. 'We must first find a place where no one will disturb us for a couple of hours.'

'What's the day today?' asked Kejriwal.

'I don't know. Friday, I guess.'

'Then I know just the place ji,' grinned Kejriwal and stepped on the accelerator.

'Welcome back, sir,' beamed the lady behind the ticket counter at PVR Saket. 'Premium lounge seats as usual?'

'*Haan ji,*' said Kejriwal.

Deve Gowda stood in front of a large poster of *Kya Kool Hain Hum 3* with a disgusted expression on his face.

'We are going to watch *this*?'

'No, 420 is going to watch it, while we enter the next dream level,' said Swamy.

'*Chhee*! This is obscene,' said Gowda, wrinkling his nose. 'I liked your dream better, Modi *avare.*'

Kejriwal immediately flared up.

'*Mein aapko bata doon, Gowdaji!*' he exclaimed, wagging a finger at Gowda. '*Yeh Kejriwal kuch bhi bardarsht kar sakta hai, lekin team ke andar rajniti nahi bardarsht karega!*'

Gowda blinked. *'Chaar run ke liye!'* he blurted, summoning all the Hindi at his command.

Inside the hall, more than a hundred AAP volunteers waited for them, with AAP leader Ashutosh at the forefront.

'What are your orders, Aravind?' asked Ashutosh, and added by habit, 'Will the Modi answer?'

'Ashu, take five to six people with you and plant explosive charges under the hall. When I give the signal, detonate them,' said Kejriwal.

'Ashu will *keel* it,' said Ashutosh and scurried off with a dozen men. The rest of the volunteers divided themselves into groups and took guard near the exits.

Meanwhile, Swamy had already got down to work. He pulled out the dream-sharing device from under one of the seats and began setting it up. Qaal-za laid out the unconscious form of the old woman on one of the seats and took the adjacent seat. Modi, Arnab, Gowda and Swamy settled in as well, stretching themselves on the luxurious pushback seats.

'This time,' said Swamy, as he pushed the button, 'we will be in Arnab's dream.'

'God knows what we will find there,' murmured Gowda.

'Shh!' urged Kejriwal, shoving a handful of popcorn into his mouth, 'the movie is starting.'

A slow smile spread across Arnab's face as he closed his eyes and slipped into unconsciousness.

An autorickshaw drove up the road outside PVR Saket and sputtered to a stop a few feet from the gate. Its driver, Lali, jumped out and stood at attention as a familiar figure emerged from the auto and squinted up at the building. From the other direction, a police jeep drove up to the auto, and out stepped another familiar face. With a curt nod at each other, Lieutenant Governor Najeeb Jung and Commissioner of Police Bhim Sain Bassi walked up to the ticket counter.

'Three tickets for *Kya Kool Hain Hum 3*, please,' said Jung.

As the woman at the ticket counter fiddled with her computer, cacophonous sounds of screeching tyres and skidding vehicles came from outside.

'I am sorry, sir, it's sold out,' the woman told the two men at the counter.

Jung and Bassi glanced at each other, then stepped aside to reveal a third man in a black suit and a dark red tie, who sauntered up to the counter.

'In that case,' said Mukesh Ambani, throwing a blank cheque at the dumbstruck woman, 'I will buy the theatre.'

A thousand Ambani agents stormed through the gates and poured into the screening hall.

On the bullet train in the first-level dream, Amit Shah stood scowling over the sleeping Kejriwal. The more he looked at him, the deeper his scowl grew, until he could no longer restrain himself. With the back of his hand, he landed a stinging slap on the Delhi CM's face. Kejriwal's face turned red, but he continued to sleep. A weight lifted off Shah's shoulders and he felt considerably lighter. Delighted, he swung back his palm to land one on his other cheek. Another few kilos lifted off his shoulders and he felt even happier. Chuckling, Shah let loose a string of rapid-fire slaps and would have continued for a long time, if not for the *thwaaackkk* he heard behind him. He swung around and saw what his brain had already told him. The projections had broken through the glass door at the end of the coach behind them and were now crowding behind the one at the end of their coach.

The first of the projections glared at Shah and rammed the sharp end of his trophy into the door. An inch-long crack appeared at the point of impact. A second projection dug his trophy into the same spot, and the crack widened to 5 inches.

Clenching his jaw, Shah reached into the back of his trousers and pulled out two handguns, one in each hand.

'My name is Amit Shah,' he said in a voice dripping with menace.

Multiple cracks had appeared on the glass door by now.

'But in the badlands of Gujarat, I have another name,' said Shah. 'They call me Encounter bhai.'

With that, Shah raised his guns and ran shooting towards the projections.

A hundred kilometres away, sixty-five present and former MPs who had written to Barack Obama in 2013 asking him not to give a visa to Narendra Modi, gathered near the bullet train tracks, a few metres ahead of a long bridge. The leader of the gang, CPI chief Sitaram Yechury, glanced at his watch, then bent down to place one ear to the track. A minute later, he rose to his feet, stepped back and pulled out a detonator device from his *jhola*. With his lips curving into a sinister smile, he hit the detonator switch and watched in smug satisfaction as a series of explosions rocked the bridge behind them and brought it down, creating a 200-metre gap in the rail link between Ahmedabad and Delhi.

TWELVE

The Nation's Dream

AN EAR-SHATTERING BOOM jolted Gowda awake. He opened his eyes and found the world on fire. An army jeep lay wrecked a few metres uphill from where he cowered, tall flames leaping from it. A hail of bullets whizzed past him, missing him by centimetres. Grenades exploded all around, kicking up walls of dust and smoke. As the utterly terrified Gowda tried to come to terms with the mayhem, the burning wreckage of the jeep toppled and started rolling down the hill, straight towards him.

'AYYO DEVRE!' shrieked Gowda, and dived to the ground. Scampering on all fours, he crawled towards a large rock nearby, dragged himself behind it and nearly cried in relief when he found Swamy already crouching there.

Overhead, a supersonic jet screamed past, leaving in its wake a thunderous crack and an air-to-surface missile that slammed into an army bunker a few hundred metres behind them with a deafening explosion, sending bits of rock and gravel flying in all directions.

'Holy Kumbhakarna! I am going deaf!' exclaimed Deve Gowda, covering his ears. 'What is all this?'

'We are in Arnab's head. What do you expect?' shouted Swamy over the din.

A few metres to their right, Modi and Qaal-za were darting through the crossfire.

'Incoming!' cried Modi as the two threw in a dive roll and crashed into Swamy and Gowda behind the rock.

For a few moments the four lay panting, telling themselves that they were still alive. When a semblance of normalcy returned to their breathing, Modi said, 'What now?'

'We need to get to that castle at the top of the hill. We will find the vault there,' said Swamy.

'How are we going to do that?' asked Modi. 'And where the hell is Arnab?'

As if on cue, the ground beneath them suddenly shuddered. With a grinding noise that drowned the roar of the gunfire, a massive Arjun tank rolled over the burning wreckage of the jeep and ground to a stop near them. The hatch flew open and out popped Arnab Goswami in a crisp black suit and aviator shades.

'Hop in,' he said, 'the nation is driving.'

Over the next hour, the tank bulldozed through the enemy's defences like they were panellists on the *Newshour*. By the time it rolled on to the top of the hill, the enemy had been vanquished and the guns had gone silent.

About 100 metres from where they stood, loomed the fortress protecting the castle they sought. The walls were heavily fortified, standing 20 feet high and 5 feet thick. A pair of thick, grey-steeled blast doors protected the entrance. Arnab turned the tank's turret towards the doors.

'We won't be able to crash through those doors,' said Swamy.

Arnab scoffed. 'The nation can,' he said, and fired. The shell slammed into the wall and exploded with a loud boom, kicking up a huge cloud of dust. After a few moments, when the air cleared, the wall was still standing, with no visible sign of damage.

'Ignoramus,' muttered Swamy.

Undeterred, Arnab fired again, with the same result. After his fourth attempt, a suspiciously familiar voice cackled through an unseen loudspeaker.

'Noise and aggression will not help you enter this compound,' the voice said in a sanctimonious tone. 'Seek a civilized debate and you shall be welcomed.'

The men conferred among themselves and decided that their only option was to accede. They abandoned the tank and stood silently before the blast doors. The ploy worked. A minute later, the doors creaked open and the men walked in.

The castle sat in the middle of the compound on a sprawling platform about 10 feet high. A thousand feet lay between them and the castle doors. And in this space, standing shoulder to shoulder, were more than a thousand junior editors, senior editors, reporters, cameramen, stringers, junior anchors and various other media personnel, all staring daggers at Arnab.

Minutes passed by as the men waited nervously for something to happen. Then, slowly, almost reluctantly, the mob parted, clearing a path that led straight to the platform.

The men exchanged anxious glances with each other, then stepped into the gap and walked towards the platform.

As they drew closer, they noticed a dozen odd figures standing on the platform in front of the doors. Rajdeep Sardesai, Karan Thapar, Shekhar Gupta, Sagarika Ghose, Barkha Dutt, Ravish Kumar, Bhupendra Chaubey and many others. Some of the most recognizable faces of Indian media. Some of the bitterest opponents of Arnab Goswami.

Behind the anchors was another set of familiar faces: Former Pakistani ambassador to India Syed Tariq Pirzada, former Pakistani diplomat Zafar Hilaly, retired admiral Javed Iqbal, Abhishek Mukherjee, Sanjay Jha, Sambit Patra, Ashutosh and a number of other prime-time regulars who had one thing in common. They were all *Newshour* bunnies who had been lambasted by Arnab at least once, and in most cases, several times.

With their footsteps echoing loudly in the silence, the group climbed the stairs to the platform. From a distant mosque, the sound of azaan rang out, amplified a split second later by a loudspeaker erected on a pole on the platform.

'This seems right out of *Gadar*,' whispered Modi.

The ornate doors of the castle were locked shut. A golden key gleamed in Barkha's hand. Above the massive doors hung a large signboard that read 'Lutyens media' in big bold letters.

For a while, the dreamers and the people on the platform stood staring at each other. Then NDTV's Ravish

Kumar spread his arms and sauntered up to Arnab with a patronizing smile.

'Bahut khush kismet ho tum Arnab Goswami, jo Lutyens media ne tumhe apni panaah mein bulaya hai!'

Ravish nodded at the castle behind him. 'You want to get in, don't you?'

Arnab nodded quietly.

Ravish's smile grew wider. 'So,' he said, 'do you accept that cacophonous and shrill TV debates are leading India into darkness?'

Arnab felt the eyes of his teammates on him and the weight of the mission on his shoulders. He quelled his natural instincts and refused to rise to the provocation. In an even tone, he said, 'This nation does not deserve candy-floss journalism. Instead it demands that as honest journalists, we ask tough questions of our leaders.'

Ravish's smile faded. 'Do you accept that noisy TV debates are plunging the nation into darkness?' he repeated, raising his voice.

Arnab fixed Ravish with an icy glare. His voice, however, remained calm. 'The true measure of a debate is the verdict the audience gives it week after week. If a channel gets the maximum viewership, it is because people feel strongly about the issues covered, and a bond has been created,' he said.

'DO YOU OR DO YOU NOT ACCEPT?'

For a fleeting moment, black rage glinted in Arnab's eyes as the anchor inside him rattled against his skin, aching to outshout the punk who had dared to raise his voice in his presence. With superhuman effort, he subdued that part of him and, through clenched teeth, muttered, 'I accept.'

A collective gasp went through the thousand mediapersons surrounding the platform. Ravish stumbled backwards in disbelief. The dozen mainstream media anchors and *Newshour* bunnies exchanged stunned glances. Did they just subdue Arnab?

Throwing his hands up in glee, Ravish exclaimed, '*Bhai wah, subhanallah! Mashallah!* Come, let's walk in together and bow down in front of Pandit Nehru's portrait.'

'One minute, Ravish!'

One man broke from the group of anchors standing on the platform and approached them. Arnab stiffened.

'Before this man is admitted into our circle,' said Rajdeep Sardesai, 'let us at least find out if he's qualified to be one of us.'

Rajdeep walked up to within a feet of Arnab and said, 'Say this, Arnab. *India Today* zindabad!'

The mob of gathered mediapersons punched the air with their fists and cried in unison, '*India Today* zindabad! *India Today* zindabad! *India Today* zindabad!'

When their cries had died down, Arnab said quietly, '*India Today* zindabad.'

'Hmm,' smirked Rajdeep. 'Say this. NDTV zindabad!'

Once again, the frenzied mob of reporters, cameramen and correspondents threw their fists up and cried, 'NDTV zindabad! NDTV zindabad! NDTV zindabad!'

Arnab bit his lip and muttered. 'NDTV zindabad.'

'Yayyyy!' roared the crowd.

The smirk on Rajdeep's face grew into a cocky grin. He exchanged triumphant nods with the other anchors before turning back to Arnab.

'Now say, *Newshour* murdabad!'

'MISTER RAJDEEP SARDESAI!'

The seismic wave that surged outwards from its epicentre in Arnab Goswami's larynx sent Rajdeep Sardesai, the anchors on the podium and the 1000-odd mediapersons staggering backwards. Birds perched on the trees in the vicinity took to the skies in droves. Dogs, goats and other animals within the radius of a kilometre scampered in terror. It was an entire minute before the echoes of 'Mister Rajdeep Sardesai' died down.

'Why this hypocrisy, Rajdeep?' demanded Arnab. 'Your *India Today*, NDTV is zindabad, I have no problems with it. But my *Newshour* was zindabad, is zindabad and will be zindabad!'

He raised a knotted fist high over his head and hollered, '*NEWSHOUR* ZINDABAD! *NEWSHOUR* ZINDABAD! *NEWSHOUR* ZINDABAD!'

'*NEWSHOUR* ZINDABAD!' cried Modi, taken in by the moment.

'*NEWSHOUR* ZINDABAD!' reiterated Arnab.

Rajdeep went purple with rage. '*Bakwaas band kar!*' he cried. 'If you want to get in, you have to say *Newshour murdabad*!'

'THAT'S ENOUGH!' bellowed back Arnab, wild tufts of hair falling across his forehead. 'IF I CAN TAKE TOUGH QUESTIONS FOR THE SAKE OF THE NATION, I CAN ALSO ASK TOUGH QUESTIONS!'

'GET HIM!' shrieked a wild-eyed Sagarika Ghose.

With an air-splitting war cry, the horde of reporters, cameramen and journalists from every channel other than Times Now sprang forward and surged towards the platform in fanatic fury, brandishing their microphones, selfie-sticks and pens like clubs, swords and daggers. Sensing the mood against their tormentor, Syed Pirzada lent his voice to the

battle cry, shook his fist and launched himself towards
Arnab, closely followed by Zafar Hilaly and other *Newshour*
bunnies. Modi, Swamy, Gowda and Qaal-za backed away
in terror as the frenzied men and women with murder in
their eyes poured towards them from every direction.

As rabid as the mob was, the expression on Arnab's face
was infinitely more maniacal. He looked left and right, then
leapt towards the nearest pole. In one motion, he ripped
the loudspeaker tied atop the pole, went down on one knee
and hollered, 'DO NOT DODGE THIS QUESTION!' right
into the faces of the first few *Newshour* bunnies to reach
him. The invisible wrecking ball that slammed into Syed
Pirzada, Zafar Hilaly and Javed Iqbal lifted them bodily
into the air and flung them 15 feet backwards. By the time
their bodies skidded to a stop, they had already passed out.
Arnab, meanwhile, had already moved on to find his next
set of victims. 'YOU HAVE BEEN EXPOSED TODAY ON
THE *NEWSHOUR!*' he bellowed through the loudspeaker
in another direction, sending an NDTV reporter skidding
backwards into a pack of advancing journalists and
scattering them like a bunch of bowling pins. Then he turned
the loudspeaker in another direction and screamed, 'THE
NATION DEMANDS AN ANSWER!' instantly flattening
two dozen marauders racing up the steps.

Amidst the pandemonium, Swamy pinched the golden
key from the hands of a shell-shocked Barkha, creaked open
the massive door and slipped in. The others quickly followed
and, just as they were pushing it shut, at the very last moment,
Arnab rolled through the gap and jumped to his feet.

'The nation is in,' he declared, adjusting his tie.

The team locked the door, barred it and pulled a heavy
piece of furniture against it.

'This won't hold them for long,' said Swamy as the mob outside pounded on the door. 'Set the charges for the kick, while I take him up to the vault.'

Swamy and the alien commander raced up the staircase, while Modi and Arnab sprinted down to the basement and began planting explosives on the pillars. Deve Gowda found himself a dark corner and sat down for a rest.

On the bullet train in the first-level dream, the first few projections that broke through the glass door received a mouthful of bullets each and fell before they could even take a step into the coach. The second wave of projections made it two steps into the coach before receiving another stream of bullets from Amit Shah's guns. The third wave of projections would have met a similar fate had Shah not run out of bullets. Five projections rushed at him with murder in their crazed eyes. Shah rammed the butts of his guns into the faces of the first two, leapt into the air and scissor-kicked the next two and simply bounced the fifth guy off his ample paunch. The first two went down like a ton of bricks. The next two crashed into the windows on the sides of the coach. The fifth went flying backwards, taking down ten other projections charging behind him.

At that point, even as the projections picked themselves up for another attack, the train's siren let out a piercing sound. Instinctively, Shah turned towards the window and saw the broken bridge 2 kilometres ahead on the curving track. Two things occurred to him instantly. The train was going to fly off the tracks in twenty-five seconds. Which meant that the kick was coming in twenty-five seconds.

As the projections prepared to charge again, Shah sprinted back towards the dreamers and slipped a pair of headphones around each of their ears.

'Hope you guys are ready,' he muttered and pushed a button on the device, playing Kejriwal's *Insaan ka insaan se ho bhaichara* on the headphones.

Just when Arvind Kejriwal was beginning to enjoy the movie and had started composing a tweet telling his followers that *Kya Kool Hain Hum 3* is a must-watch, he was rudely interrupted by a loud commotion. He looked up and nearly choked on his popcorn. Scores of Ambani agents were scuffling with his volunteers all around him and, by the looks of it, getting the better of them. He watched in horror as more Ambani agents poured in through the exits, heavily outnumbering the volunteers.

Six volunteers broke away from the fighting and took position around Kejriwal.

'I don't need any security,' exclaimed Kejriwal, pushing them away. 'God will protect me. Go!'

At that moment, he heard something awful ringing in his ears. It took him a second to realize it was his own voice singing his favourite song. It took him another second to realize that it was time for the kick.

From the exit behind Kejriwal, LG Jung, Police Commissioner Bassi and Mukesh Ambani sauntered in unchallenged along with two dozen Ambani agents. Spotting the unprotected Kejriwal five rows below them, they split into three groups and converged on him from three different directions.

'ASHU! NOW!' cried Kejriwal as the men grabbed him and hauled him away bodily.

Watching the projections take his beloved leader, Ashu wailed, 'Why are you all scared of the Kajariwal? Will the Modi answer?'

Sobbing clownishly, he pushed down the detonator switch, and the theatre exploded.

'What's in there?' asked a nervous Qaal-za.

Swamy regarded the glimmering stainless steel doors of the vault. 'Hopefully, the secret the old woman does not want you to learn.'

With a tentative hand, Qaal-za reached for the keypad and typed in 628466, spelling out 'nation'. The locking mechanism snapped open and the doors of the vault slowly slid aside.

Qaal-za stepped in and found himself in a closed backyard behind a non-descript two-storeyed house. Tall trees bordered the yard. There was no one in sight. Everything was quiet, except for the rustling of leaves in the gentle breeze.

A pile of wreckage sat in the middle of the yard. It appeared to be that of a vehicle of some kind. The body was smashed out of shape, the chassis, burnt and battered. Charred debris lay scattered around it. The vehicle, whatever it was, was damaged beyond recognition.

But the alien commander recognized it instantly. It was the same space shuttle that had carried the alien prince out into space on that fateful day all those years ago. A cold hand clamped his heart. He stumbled forward, brushing his trembling fingers against the torn hull of the shuttle. An unspeakable fear gripped his soul as he walked around the wreckage. His heart beat faster and faster.

In the front portion of the wrecked shuttle was a charred skeleton sitting in a pool of smouldering alien blood. A red pendant lay beside the skeleton, broken in two.

A despairing wail escaped Qaal-za's lips. His knees buckled and he collapsed to the ground. 'My prince . . . my prince . . .' he sobbed inconsolably.

Watching the sobbing alien commander from near the vault's door, Swamy nodded in satisfaction. Kejriwal's cacophonous rendition of *Insaan ka insaan se ho bhaichara* was ringing in his ears. It was time for the kick. Swamy pulled out the detonator and placed a thumb over the switch.

The weeping alien commander sobbed for several minutes. When he could cry no more, he sat up and stared ahead with an utterly disconsolate expression.

'I have failed,' he mumbled. 'My prince is gone. What am I supposed to do here now?'

Swamy nodded again. The inception was working. They were so close . . .

'I will return to Mor . . .'

Yes! Swamy's heart leapt in joy. The plan had worked! He slammed down the detonator switch.

A dozen near-simultaneous explosions rocked the castle's basement, blasting the pillars supporting the building to smithereens. Section by section, the floors collapsed, starting with the part near the door. Modi and Arnab fell along with the collapsing floor and awoke in the cinema hall in the second-level dream just as the floor under them gave away.

'What about Mister Gowda?' shouted Arnab as they fell through the collapsing floor.

'The projections have taken AK49, which means he's in limbo. Gowdaji will find him and bring him back,' shouted back Modi, just before they awoke in the bullet train in freefall.

Back in the disintegrating third-level dream, as the castle collapsed all around him, Swamy frowned. The despair on Qaal-za's countenance had vanished. In its place, something else had taken root. Rage.

'I will return to Mor . . .' Qaal-za repeated, his features dark and foreboding, '. . . but not before making the people responsible pay dearly.'

'What?' blurted Swamy.

The alien commander rose to his feet and raised a gnarled fist. 'In the name of my fallen prince, I vow today that I will destroy this country. I will turn all Indian citizens including illegal Bangladeshi immigrants into mindless zombies. By the time I am done, this place will be known as Zombieland.'

That was the last thing Swamy saw before he fell through the ground, rode the kick all the way up and woke up back in 7, RCR's master bedroom, realizing that the situation was now way worse than before.

THIRTEEN

Alien-Mukt Bharat

EXACTLY ONE HUNDRED and eighty minutes after Dr Manmohan Singh carpet-bombed Qaal-za's security apparatus with his economics mumbo jumbo, the elite alien soldiers lying sprawled on the lawns of 7, RCR began to stir. One by one they sat up groggily and looked at each other with bleary eyes. At once they remembered the events leading to their sudden spell of slumber and sprang to their feet. Some of them positioned themselves along the bungalow's perimeter, while the rest stormed the house through the main door.

Inside the bungalow's master bedroom, Swamy leapt from the bed.

'We need to get out of here before ET wakes up,' said Swamy.

'What happened?' asked Modi.

'The inception worked. ET is convinced that his prince is dead.'

'That's great! So he's going back immediately, right?'
'No.'
'What! Why not?'
'He now blames us for killing his prince. The rascal wants to destroy you and turn this country into zombieland.'
Modi winced.
'As if we didn't have enough people wanting to do that,' he muttered.
The four men rolled the sleeping Kejriwal and Gowda under the bed, exited the room and locked it shut. Then they took off running down the corridor, towards the back entrance. Just as they turned into the portion of the house leading to the back door, it crashed open and three alien soldiers led by alien captain Saal-fa sprang in, forcing the four men to turn back and flee down the same path.
'What do we do now? We are trapped!' exclaimed Shah.
'I know a way out. Come on, mitron!' said Modi.
Dodging the shots fired by the pursuing aliens, Modi led the men into his walk-in wardrobe and locked the door behind them. He walked over to the shelf showcasing his headgears and tapped on the beak of a traditional hornbill hat of Arunachal Pradesh. The back of the shelf shifted backwards, revealing a secret passage about 3 feet wide.
'I use it during emergencies,' Modi explained to his astonished teammates.
The four men sprinted down the passage for several minutes, until a dim light appeared in the distance. Moments later, the passage opened into what seemed like the back of an apparel showroom. Rows and rows of shirts, suits, jackets and kurtas were on display. A man with a measuring tape around his neck turned towards them and beamed.

'Oh welcome back, Modiji!' he said cheerfully. 'What is it today? Half-sleeved kurta? Business suit? Nehru jacket?'

'Go home, Bipin bhai. It's not safe,' said Modi and walked out of the shop.

Back in 7, RCR, captain Saal-fa kicked open the door to the master bedroom and walked in to find a livid Qaal-za sitting on the bed.

'Order our troops to attack the humans,' said the alien commander in a voice trembling with anger. 'Shoot everyone.'

In the war room of a Pakistani forward base near Lahore, an anxious General Sharif pored over a large map spread out on his desk, along with his corps commanders.

Things had not gone as per his plan. The Indians had mobilized way too quickly. Their divisions had deployed much too accurately. Almost as if they had known beforehand what they were up to. The element of surprise he had hoped for was lost. His forces were now evenly matched, possibly even outmatched. His best-laid plans had gone awry. He couldn't believe it.

But then, that's exactly why he was different from his predecessors. He had a contingency plan, which was really his trump card. He had the aliens. Saal-fa's spaceships would make all the difference.

With that, he dialled the alien captain's number on the field telephone in the room.

'Captain Saal-fa, this is General Sharif. We are all set to strike. Are you ready for us?'

'Yes, General Sharif,' replied Saal-fa. 'Our ships are currently on standby in a geostationary orbit. We can get them to the warzone in two hours.'

'Fantastic!'

'We will have to time this well. I suggest you launch your attack right away. I'll call in sixty minutes for the precise coordinates. Over and out.'

General Sharif replaced the receiver with a smile and turned to his corps commanders.

'Launch the offensive.'

It started in the cities—Delhi, Mumbai, Bengaluru, Chennai, Hyderabad, Kolkata and many others. Alien soldiers patrolling the streets, sipping tea at roadside tea stalls, smoking cigarettes and chit-chatting with shopkeepers were suddenly asked to report back to their units. Fifteen minutes later, they returned to their positions with raised guns and grim expressions. Without warning, the aliens started firing at the humans, instantly turning them into zombies.

After thirty seconds of firing by the aliens, the population of zombies in India crossed that of the Parsis. After half an hour, zombies outnumbered the Jains in India. After one hour, there were more zombies than Buddhists in the country. By noon, zombies were a vote bank.

Streets were rife with wooden-faced zombies aimlessly plodding up and down. Traffic came to a standstill. Cars were strewn here and there with blank-faced drivers still sitting in them. Colonies wore a deserted look as terrified humans locked themselves up in their homes or took their families and fled. Fighting back was futile, as some discovered in the brief moments before they were turned into zombies. Bullets, sharp objects, stones, black ink, whatever the humans threw at the aliens simply bounced off the translucent shields around them.

Despite the systematic operation by the aliens, they were far fewer in number, and there were way too many humans for them to zombify in such a short time. Thousands escaped, finding hiding spots untouched by aliens. Pockets of human resistance began to emerge in a handful of buildings and fortified open spaces.

The largest such sanctuary was at the Ramlila Maidan in Delhi, where the high, fortified walls and cast-iron gates gave an illusion of safety, no matter how temporary.

So when word reached Modi that more than 10,000 men, women and children had gathered in Ramlila Maidan, he saw in it a sign from the gods. For it was there that his journey from a BJP strongman to the prime minister of this great nation began. So what if it was Anna Hazare who kick-started it.

Without a second thought, the four men made straight for Ramlila Maidan.

Away from the unfolding chaos, in the quiet of Qaal-za's spaceship, Sonia Gandhi stepped towards one of the portholes and cautiously peeped through it. Finding nothing other than an empty airstrip, she exhaled in relief and allowed herself to relax. Her adrenaline rush receded, leaving her suddenly exhausted. She turned to check on Rahul Gandhi and found him sitting on his haunches, carefully arranging a handful of marbles on the floor. Figuring that they were safe

for the time being, she decided to find a place to rest. One of
the doors in the room opened into a snug sleeping chamber.
She flopped on to the inviting bed and went out like a light.

A cloud of desolation hung over Ramlila Maidan. People
sat scattered all over the grounds, scared and exhausted, as
they cowered in small groups, holding each other's hands,
drawing their young ones closer. Those BJP workers and
leaders who had managed to escape the aliens were sprawled
on one side, saffron flags and banners lying in the dirt. AAP
workers and leaders sat elsewhere, similarly deflated, grimy
AAP hats sitting crooked on their heads. There were a few
dozen Congress workers too, looking even more empty and
discouraged than usual.

Wherever Modi looked, he saw defeat and resignation.
Wherever he turned, there was an overwhelming sense of
hopelessness.

He remembered one other time when this had
happened . . .

And just like that, his doubts were gone. No longer
did he need counsel. No longer did he have to depend on
others' abilities. He knew exactly what he had to do. This
was familiar. This was in his hitting zone. This was what he
was born for.

And so, Narendra Damodardas Modi grabbed a
microphone and climbed atop an abandoned fish cart to
deliver the most important speech of his life.

'*Bharat mata ki* . . .' he rumbled.

The chatter in the grounds went silent. Heads turned. A
few BJP workers sat up with sudden interest once they saw

who was on the fish cart. Shah and Swamy climbed on to the fish cart behind Modi, raised their fists and said 'Jai!' Arnab pulled out his smartphone and began filming.

Modi rumbled again, '*Bharat mata ki . . .*'

More BJP workers in the maidan sat up straight. Some jumped to their feet. A few raised their banners and joined the answering cry of 'Jai!'

Modi surveyed his audience with the slow, measured sweep that is a hallmark of his election rally speeches. Behind him on the fish cart, Shah pulled out a device from his pocket and pressed a button on it. Across the country, hundreds of 3D holograms of Modi began to pop up in prominent places—at Mumbai's Gateway of India, under the Charminar in Hyderabad, on Chennai's Marina Beach, in Patna's Gandhi Maidan, at Bengaluru's iconic Silk Board junction and a dozen other cities. TV channels that were still running cut live to Ramlila Maidan. Radio channels followed suit, terming it a special broadcast of *Mann ki baat*. Within minutes, Modi was on every TV screen, every radio channel, every street, every town and every city.

At Ramlila Maidan, there was now pin-drop silence.

'*Manch par viraajman,*' began Modi, '*Bharatiya Janata Party ke adhyaksha . . . Shri Amit bhai Shah . . . Bharatiya Janata Party ke varisht mahanuvhav anti-corruption crusader . . . Shri Subramanian Swamy ji aur mere desh ke sava sau crore bhaiyon aur behnon!*'

One by one, people moved from their spots and inched closer to the fish cart. Word of Modi's presence spread and a steady stream of people began to pour in through the gates.

'*Bhaiyon aur behnon, aaj mein aap ke paas rone dhone ke liye nahi aaya hoon,*' said Modi. '*Na mein aansu bahaane aaya hoon. Na hi mein aansu bahaane waalon ki katha sunaane aaya hoon.'*

Modi raised his forefinger. *'Mein aaj yahaan pe aaya hoon . . . aap ke aansu pochne ka vishwaas dene ke liye!'*

By now the grounds were jam-packed. Side by side in the crowded arena, people of all ages stood cheek by jowl, eyes only for the man on the fish cart.

'Mitron, kya haalat kar diya inn aliens ne!' cried Modi, his expression a perfect blend of anger and pain. *'Aaj gareeb zombie ban kar ke ghoom raha hai! Uske biwi bachche aansu pee ke so rahe hain! Kisaan ke khet mein aliens ke spaceship baithe hain! Baevas ho kar ke woh aatmahatya kar leta hai!'*

Modi let that sink in for a few moments, after which he leaned forward in a conspiratorial tone and said, *'Mitron, Delhi ki sultanate ko vikaas karne ki ruchi nahi hai. Unhe sirf apna pet bharne se matlab hai.'*

Then it happened.

It began like a whisper somewhere amidst the vast sea of people on the grounds, and grew louder by the second as more and more people picked it up, until almost the entire maidan was chanting in unison.

'Modi . . . Modi . . . Modi!'

Shah and Swamy squeezed each other's hands in feverish excitement. 'He's still got it,' whispered Shah.

'Mitron, mein aap se ek sawaal poochna chahta hoon. Jawaab doge?' demanded Modi, pointing a forefinger to one section of the crowd.

'Haan!' the crowd replied.

'Jawaab doge?' he repeated, pointing his finger at another part of the crowd.

'Haan!'

'*Ek mahine pehle, Qaal-za ne Modi se haath mila kar, Bharat ke vikaas ke liye madad karne ka vaada kiya tha?*'

'*Haan!*'

'*Vikaas hua?*'

'*Nahi!*'

'*Bhaiyon aur behnon,*' said Modi in a declaratory tone, '*Qaal-za ne vishwaas ghaat Modi se nahi kiya hai . . . vishwaas ghaat Bharat ke koti koti jano se kiya hai! Yeh vishwaas ghaat aap ke saath hai!*'

He sensed that it was time to shift gears.

'*Yeh vishwaas ghaat karne waalon ko saza doge?*'

'*Haan!*' the crowd screamed back.

'*Yeh vishwaas ghaat karne waalon ko saza doge?*'

'*Haan!!*'

'*Yeh vishwaas ghaat karne waalon ko ukhaad kar phek doge?*'

'*Haan!!!*'

Modi went for the kill.

'*Bhaiyon aur behnon! Mahatma Gandhi ne Champaran mein Angrez-mukt Bharat ki baat kahi thi. Sau saal baad, maine Patna ke Gandhi Maidan mein Congress-mukt Bharat ki baat kahi thi. Aaj, yahan Ramlila Maidan se goonjna chahiye . . . ALIEN-MUKT BHARAT!*'

The roar that followed brought Ramlila Maidan down.

Rahul Gandhi frowned at the two marbles still in the 2-foot-wide circle he had scratched on the ship's floor.

'Modi?' he murmured, pointing a finger at the marble on the left, 'or Kejriwal?' he added, shifting his finger to point at the other. 'Who do I take out first?'

He scratched his stubble absently, pondering over the dilemma. As seconds turned into minutes, tension began to build within him and the responsibility of the decision began to weigh heavily upon his shoulders. For a brief moment he entertained thoughts of giving up and going on a vacation. Then, mustering all the resolve at his command, he willed his mind to focus on the challenge and, after a few more minutes of deliberation, made his decision.

He went down on his knees and placed his right thumb on the floor. Brows furrowed in concentration, he set a marble against his right forefinger, pulled it back as far as he could and released it. The marble catapulted from his finger and collided head-on with the marble on the left, knocking it out of the circle.

'In your face, you suit-boot *ka* marble!' he whooped in delight.

Two hours later, after having played the game a few more times, Rahul got bored. He had nothing else, neither his spinning top nor his action figures to distract himself with. In their hurry to flee 10, Janpath, he hadn't had the chance to grab anything.

For a while, he amused himself making fart sounds with his armpits, then soon got tired of that as well. That's when he decided to explore the spaceship.

Modi sipped from a glass of water, then swept the maidan with his gaze once again, waiting for the 'Modi! Modi!' chants to abate. He noticed that two spots in the crowd weren't as ebullient as the rest. One of those groups wore the white hats of AAP, while the other carried tricolour flags with the Congress hand in place of the chakra. It was time to unfurl the statesman in him.

'*Bhaiyon aur behnon!*' Modi resumed with vigour, '*Mein mere BJP ke karyakarta se poochna chahta hoon . . . mein mere Congress ke karyakarta se poochna chahta hoon . . . aaj, tumhe ek doosre se ladna hai? Ki saath mil kar ke aliens se ladna hai?*'

'Aliens!' the crowd cried.

'*Mein mere desh ke AAPtard se poochna chahta hoon . . . mein mere desh ke bhakt se poochna chahta hoon . . . aaj, tumhe ek doosre ko troll karna hai ki saath mil kar ke aliens ko troll karna hai?*'

'Aliens!' the crowd reiterated.

'*Bhaiyon aur behnon! Congress ka karyakarta aliens se ladna chahta hai. BJP ka karyakarta bhi aliens se ladna chahta hai. AAPtard aliens se ladna chahta hai. Bhakt bhi aliens se ladna chahta hai. Aao, hum sab mil kar ke, aliens ko khatam karte hain!*'

Then Modi did the unthinkable.

He had worn all kinds of headgear onstage. He had worn the Sikh's turban, the hornbill hat of Arunachal Pradesh, the *Kung-Fu Panda*-style Jaapi hat of Assam, the colourful safa of Rajasthan, an assortment of saffron turbans and several other traditional headgear. He had even pranced around Sabarmati riverfront wearing a cowboy hat once. But never had he worn *that* cap.

Shah goggled in astonishment as Modi put on the '*Mein aam aadmi hoon, mujhe chahiye Swaraj*' cap popularized by the Aam Aadmi Party. On the ground, the eyes of the AAP workers lit up.

Modi then reached for his second *brahmastra*.

'*Ek alien-mukt Bharat ke sapne ko saakaar karne ke liye, aaj iss manch par, mein Rajiv Gandhi Alien Fightback Yojana ki ghoshna karta hoon!*'

Like a spell that raises the dead, the magic words brought the dispirited Congress workers to life and, along with their AAP counterparts, they stood one by one and joined the rest of the crowd in the 'Modi! Modi!' chants.

Modi raised a fist. '*Ab ki baar . . . ?*' he roared.

The crowd roared back, 'Modi *sarkar!*'

'Na, na,' said Modi. '*Mein bolunga "Ab ki baar", aap jawaab do "Aliens pe vaar". Bologe?*'

'*Haan!*' came the reply.

'*Bologe?*'

'*Haan!*'

'*Ab ki baar!*'

'*Aliens pe vaar!*' roared Ramlila Maidan.

'*Ab ki baar!*'

'*Aliens pe vaar!*'

Modi was now in the home stretch. Raising both fists high over his head, he cried, '*Dono mutthi upar kar zor se bolo . . . Vande!*'

'*Mataram!*'

'*Vande!*'

'*Mataram!*'

'*Vande! Vande! Vande!*'

'*Mataram! Mataram! Mataram!*'

And once again, hope soared in the hearts of the people of India, belief returned to their battered souls, and they found in themselves the strength to face yet another thing thrown at them in this great country.

Just in time too. For the uproar at Ramlila Maidan had caught the attention of a battalion of alien soldiers who poured through the two gates and spread themselves around the grounds to surround the crowd.

The leader of the alien battalion stepped forward a few paces and flashed an arrogant grin at the men on the fish cart.

Modi's expression hardened. He extended his right palm, on which Amit Shah placed a *trishul*. Then, like an Olympic javelin thrower, Modi jumped out with his left leg and flung the trishul high into the air.

The alien leader's grin widened as the trishul soared through the sky in a parabolic trajectory. He blew Modi an air kiss, then turned around, pulled down his pants and wiggled his backside, secure in the knowledge that the missile would bounce off his shield like everything else.

As the trishul curved downwards and its gleaming tips tore inexorably towards the alien leader's jiggling grey bottom, a billion humans held their breath, for the next moment would determine their fate on this planet.

FOURTEEN

Sava Sau Crore People Fight Back

RAHUL GANDHI WAS having the time of his life exploring Qaal-za's ship.

'Whoopieee!' he squealed as he dashed down another corridor.

After one hour of pushing through unopened doors, squeezing through hatches and tinkering with strange equipment, he came across a pair of shiny metallic doors, bigger and wider than any other he had seen so far on the ship.

His curiosity piqued, Rahul tried pushing the door. It wouldn't budge. He jammed his fingers in the thin crevice between the two halves of the door and tried to pry them open. Same result.

Frowning, he stepped back. His eyes fell on a numeric keypad adjacent to the door and his frown deepened. He rubbed his chin and stared at the keypad.

Inspiration struck and his eyes lit up. He sprang forward and began typing out multiplication tables on the keypad.

'Two ones are two, two twos are four, two threes are six . . .' he recited, typing in 2102, 2104, 2106 one after the other. Each time, the keypad beeped and flashed red, indicating a denial of access. Rahul, however, paid no attention to it, moving on to the table of three when he was done with two, and then to four, five and six. '. . . Six threes are eighteen, six fours are twenty-four, six fives are thirty . . .'

Midway through the table of nine, the keypad suddenly flashed green and made a different sound. Rahul jumped back as the doors slid open, revealing a room filled with consoles, monitors, control panels, levers and a giant black screen.

'Wowwie!' exclaimed Rahul, wide-eyed.

He wandered in, gazing around in awe, feeling very much like a kid in a candy store, wondering which joystick, switch, or console to tinker with first. His eyes fell on the largest lever in the room. With an excited squeal, he darted towards it and pulled it down with all his strength.

The spaceship woke up with a dull buzzing sound. The panels came alive with hundreds of small flickering lights. Bright and dark globules of varying sizes started appearing on the giant black screen. Then, to Rahul's utmost delight, the spaceship lifted from the ground and began to rise into the sky.

Ten minutes into the spacecraft's ascent, a display screen in the corner of the control room flickered. The left half of the screen had a map of India on it, with tens of thousands of green dots scattered within the boundaries of the country. The right half displayed a three-dimensional wireframe image of an alien body with a shimmering layer of translucence around its outline.

A minute later, the shimmering translucent layer around the alien wireframe suddenly disappeared. Then, the green dots on the India map began to turn red one by one, until there wasn't a single green dot left and the shield controller's link with the tens of thousands of aliens on the ground was severed completely.

One instant the alien leader was grinning from ear to ear. The next second, a 5-foot-long trishul buried itself into his backside.

'OOOH!' the crowd grimaced collectively.

'YESSS!' Modi, Shah and Swamy pumped their fists in unison.

'UI MAAAAAA!' the alien leader screamed.

Several things happened in the moments that followed. First, the humans realized that the aliens were no longer invincible. Second, the aliens realized that the humans had realized they were no longer invincible. Third, high-definition footage and images of the precise juncture when the trishul rammed into the alien leader's posterior was instantly broadcast to several million households across the nation. Fourth, these images then made their way to social media in the form of updates, tweets and memes, fashioned as per the political biases of the poster or tweeter. BJP supporters posted the images with captions such as 'This is how a 56-inch PM works!' and 'If this is not *Achhe din*, what is?' Congress supporters posted the same images with captions such as 'This is how Modi deals with dissent!'

and 'Minorities under attack by Modi!' AAP supporters posted them with captions such as 'Why is Modi attacking honest aliens? Is he scared of them?' and '#12thpassModi attacks alien for raising questions about his fake degree'. Fifth, netizens across the country liked, shared, retweeted, favourited and WhatsApped these updates like there was no tomorrow, which was an actual possibility this time.

By the time the alien leader's unconscious body stopped twitching on the hard ground of Ramlila Maidan, the entire nation knew that they could now hurt the aliens.

'MAARO SAALON KO!' cried someone at Ramlila Maidan.

With a roar that shook the very ground beneath them, the humans charged at the aliens in mad fury. The aliens gawked in astonishment. Then they too let out a collective otherworldly war cry and charged at the humans, firing indiscriminately.

Watching the maidan plunge into violent chaos, Modi, Shah and Swamy stepped off the fish cart.

'Uh, I think we better get out of here,' said Shah, backing away towards the east gate.

Arnab, on the other hand, flung his camera away and took off towards the heart of the battle, screaming, 'THE NATION WILL JOIN THIS DEBATE!'

The aliens were vicious, their weapons lethal. But they were no match for a horde of angry Dilliwaalas. Inch by inch, the humans pushed them back and, within minutes, the balance of the battle began to tilt towards the humans. Before long, the aliens found themselves with their backs against the wall.

And then, the west gate flew open. Five thousand roaring alien soldiers poured in and suddenly, there were as many aliens as there were humans. Buoyed by the reinforcements, those pinned against the walls began fighting with renewed vigour.

Fifty feet above the dust and din of battle, riding on the landing skids of an attack helicopter piloted by captain Saal-fa, came alien commander Qaal-za. Even as his men pressed back the humans on ground, the alien commander scanned the battlefield systematically.

'There!' he cried, pointing directly at Modi, Shah and Swamy.

'Uh-oh,' said Modi as the attack helicopter swerved towards them.

'Run!' exclaimed Shah.

With bullets peppering their trail, the three men scampered out of the east gate and jumped into an abandoned Uber taxi. Shah shoved the driver-turned-zombie out and took the wheel. Three seconds later, the car was hurtling down Asif Ali Road with the helicopter in hot pursuit.

Approximately 80 kilometres south of Lahore, Pakistan's 1st Armoured Division emerged from its camouflage in the Changa Manga forest and rolled across the border along with the 14th Infantry Division and the 40th Infantry Division, slicing through Indian defences with ease. Simultaneously, the I Corps and the IV Corps led the charge across the border down south in Punjab and up north in Jammu and Kashmir. For a while, it seemed like the shock-and-awe blitzkrieg tactic was working. The Strike Corps easily overwhelmed Indian defences and made rapid inroads into Indian territory.

'We may not need the aliens after all,' exclaimed General Sharif as the men in the Pakistani war room whooped and high-fived each other.

Then, the Pakistani 1st Armoured Division ran into the Indian 1st Armoured Division of the II Corps. Within the span of an hour, the tide of the battle turned as the numerically superior Indian forces counter-attacked aggressively and stemmed the Pakistani charge. The other two Pakistani Strike Corps were similarly challenged by Indian Corps, and soon, the scenario began to look rather different from that at the start of the battle.

'Er, General, we may have celebrated too early,' said a nervous Lieutenant General Zubair Hayat. 'Our troops are facing heavy resistance on all fronts. The I Corps is barely holding. On the other two fronts, we are already being pushed back.'

General Sharif bit his lip. His eyes flicked to the clock. There was still some time to go for Saal-fa's call, but Sharif decided to ring the alien captain up anyway.

'The subscriber is not reachable at the moment,' said a lady in a pleasant voice.

After two more attempts, General Sharif cursed under his breath and replaced the receiver.

For the next two hours, as the situation on the battlefield steadily turned worse, the top military leaders of Pakistan sat around the table, staring at the phone. When the phone finally rang, General Sharif leapt from his seat and grabbed the receiver before it could complete its first ring.

'Ya Allah! You called just in time, Captain Saal-fa,' he exclaimed breathlessly, 'the coordinates are . . .'

'*Haan, namashkar ji! Kaise hain aap?*' replied a familiar voice. '*Mein Arvind Kejriwal bol raha hoon. Bas ek minute baat karni hai, phone mat kaatiyega . . .*'

General Sharif's eyes widened. His hands began to tremble and his mouth opened and closed soundlessly. Then he dropped to his knees and screamed, 'NOOOOOOOOOOOOOOO!'

Within an hour of the first blows being exchanged in Ramlila Maidan, spontaneous riots broke out at a hundred different places across India, and soon, the country was in the grip of an all-out war.

The first to take the attack to the aliens in Chennai were the auto drivers. For the first time in the history of Chennai, they dropped off their passengers without squeezing them out of every penny they owned, and swaggered menacingly towards the aliens to the beats of the soundtrack from Rajinikanth-starrer *Baasha*. What followed was right out of a South Indian movie or a Rohit Shetty action flick. Isaac Newton turned in his grave as the auto-walas, demonstrating the same contempt for physics that they reserve for fair pricing, punched and roundhouse-kicked alien soldiers by the dozen, sending them flying high into the air.

Then the citizens got into the act. The young took out their *aruvals*, hoisted up their lungis and charged out of their homes, screaming vernacular expletives at the aliens. The old went up to their terraces and dropped Amma mixer-grinders and DMK colour TV sets on the unsuspecting aliens.

Watching their voters take on the aliens with gusto, the politicians decided that it might be a good idea to jump in, given that elections were round the corner. An urgent meeting was called between followers of Stalin and Alagiri. The two factions decided on a temporary truce and joined hands to take on the aliens. Armed with DMK supremo

M. Karunanidhi's blessings and the wisdom of a handful of Thirukkurals, they pounced on the aliens with enthusiasm.

Elsewhere, DMDK party workers pinned down alien soldiers one by one and water-boarded them with desi liquor, while a delirious Captain Vijayakanth, swaying unsteadily on his feet, ranted about something that was understood neither by the aliens nor by the humans.

The biggest blow to Chennai's aliens was delivered by Amma's workers. Led by O. Panneerselvam, Amma's loyal workers chased down the terrified aliens, held them down and stuck Amma's stickers and posters all over their faces and bodies. When they were through, hundreds of mummified aliens lay prostrate in front of a life-size poster of a smiling Amma.

The few aliens who managed to survive all this were hit by rumours that Rajinikanth might join the human counter-attack, upon which they promptly jumped into the Bay of Bengal and drowned themselves.

The commercial capital of India witnessed an astonishing phenomenon. Over a thousand workers from MNS and Shiv Sena gathered in Mumbai's Azad Maidan and shook hands with each other. An even more astonishing development followed. The two groups walked over together to a bunch of incredulous Bihari labourers and hugged them. After that, the aliens stood no chance. From Borivali in the north to Colaba in the south, aliens were thrashed, their faces blackened and their spaceships vandalized.

After that, regular Mumbaikars from different walks of life chipped in. Dabbawalas wearing noise-cancelling headphones raced through the city's streets carrying boom boxes playing *Newshour* episodes at full volume, causing widespread alien fatalities and some human collateral damage. Aliens unfortunate enough to hang around on platforms of Mumbai's suburban railway network were shoved into hyper-crowded locals by passengers and had the air squeezed out of them. Some parts of Mumbai became so crowded that aliens ran out of land to stand on and began toppling into the sea.

The police department of Haryana beat all the other state police forces in terms of its contribution to the war on the aliens. They simply released the 400-odd Jats arrested after the first Jat agitation. These Jats got together with a thousand more Jats and went on another rampage across Haryana. While there was not much destruction of property this time, mostly because almost all of it had been destroyed in the previous agitation, hundreds of aliens perished in the crossfire.

AIMIM leader Akbaruddin Owaisi told a mob of wild-eyed supporters in Hyderabad that the aliens' shields were down for fifteen minutes, and that it was time for the Muslims to show their strength. With a bloodthirsty roar, the mob poured out into the streets of Hyderabad and thrashed the daylights out of every alien they found.

Similar scenes unfolded in the rest of the country. Aliens in Madhya Pradesh were bumped off after someone spread rumours that they were witnesses in the Vyapam scam. Aliens in Uttar Pradesh were beaten up by SP goondas and trampled on by Azam Khan's buffaloes. Aliens in West Bengal were clobbered by CPM and TMC goondas. A clever few tried to pass themselves off as Indians by showing their Aadhar cards, but they fooled no one and were promptly walloped. Aliens in Odisha were washed away by a sudden cyclone that came out of nowhere. Aliens in Bengaluru were roughed up by angry motorists stuck in traffic.

The fiercest fighting was seen in the National Capital Region, where the concentration of the aliens was the highest. Political leaders, party workers, media personnel and ordinary citizens kept aside their differences, biases and pettiness, and jumped into the battle with a sense of shared purpose.

Outside the India Today office in Noida, Rajdeep Sardesai was single-handedly taking on a swarm of aliens with a little help from a Twitter troll who hid behind a bush nearby and kept yelling 'Newstrader' every few seconds.

'Did Modi tell you to attack us?' Rajdeep shouted at a bewildered alien and knocked him cold with a jab-cross-left-hook combo.

'Did Modi tell you to invade us?' he demanded of another alien and followed it up with a jab-cross-left-hook-right-uppercut combo.

Ten minutes later, Rajdeep knocked out the last remaining alien and stood growling over him like Muhammad Ali had stood over Sonny Liston in that legendary 1965 boxing match. By then, the Twitter troll had safely made his escape.

Elsewhere in NCR, a shirtless Robert Vadra worked his abs in the Habitat Centre gym, punching a dazed alien held up by his spotter every time he completed a sit-up.

'Are you serious? Four hundred and eighteen!' grunted Vadra and punched the alien. 'Are you serious? Four hundred and nineteen! Are you serious? Four hundred and twenty!'

Somewhere in south Delhi, a group of volunteers led by AAP leader Somnath Bharti moved from one alien unit to another, roughing them up with sticks and collecting their urine samples. Inside the JNU campus, Kanhaiya Kumar and his gang of Left-leaning sloganeers dragged in aliens from the vicinity and beat them up senseless, while batchmates around them screamed, '*Alienvaad se . . . azaadi!*'

Delhi's citizenry too rose to the occasion. Rich dads threw their car keys to their spoilt teenage kids and asked them to let it rip. Within minutes, scores of Mercedes, BMWs, Audis and even a couple of Rolls-Royces were seen speeding all over the city. Familiar with such sights, Delhiites wisely stayed away from the roads and the pedestrian walks. The aliens patrolling the streets didn't and were mowed down mercilessly by the killer vehicles.

It was the Delhi Jal Board, though, that engineered a catatonic shift in the battle. Under cover of the unfolding chaos, a team of engineers spread out to various treatment plants in the NCR region and shut them down. An hour later, when households across Delhi turned on their taps, they received something that was potentially harmful to the human body, but would prove to be absolutely fatal to the alien body chemistry—untreated Yamuna water.

News quickly spread from housewife to housewife, neighbour to neighbour, and soon, men, women, boys and girls began filling buckets, mugs, pots, utensils and any container they could find with lethal water from their taps. Like defenders of a besieged citadel pouring boiling water over enemy soldiers, they drenched the aliens crawling up their walls with the dreaded Yamuna water and watched in glee as the shrieking aliens burned and disintegrated in front of their eyes.

The coup de grace was delivered by the farmers of Punjab who waded into their farms en masse and set fire to their crop, generating a humongous volume of smoke that drifted eastwards towards Delhi. Simultaneously, truck drivers from Rajasthan, Haryana, Punjab, Himachal

Pradesh and Uttar Pradesh all made a beeline towards Delhi, and drove in circles within NCR. The diesel fumes from the trucks coupled with the smoke from Punjab combined with the cool winter air to produce the mother of all smogs. Even as humans rushed to the relative safety of their apartments, aliens all across Delhi instantly doubled over in pain, coughing uncontrollably. Before long, their lungs collapsed under the onslaught and the aliens met their grisly end.

The attack helicopter piloted by Saal-fa targeted the taxi with an unending stream of bullets as it pursued it over flyovers, between skyscrapers and even through the occasional tunnel. Incredibly, not one bullet hit the taxi. Swerving, skidding and drifting like a professional racer, Amit Shah headed east at a red-hot pace.

'Where did you learn to drive like this?' shouted Modi, desperately clinging to the overhead handle with both hands.

'In Gujarat, saheb, while we were keeping an eye on . . .'

'Never mind,' Modi said hurriedly.

Unfortunately, Shah's luck did not last long. Just as the taxi climbed on to the Old ITO Bridge over the Yamuna River, an air-to-surface missile fired by the helicopter took out a portion of the bridge ahead. Shah braked hard and the taxi veered out of control. Round and round it spun, before toppling over and coming to a stop inches short of the edge of the bridge.

'What do we do, sir?' said Lieutenant Hayat.

General Sharif stared sullenly at the phone. Five hours had passed. It was official. Saal-fa wasn't calling. The aliens weren't coming. They were on their own.

'We are getting humped left, right and centre, sir. Our condition is really bad,' said Hayat.

General Sharif blanched. He sat back in his seat and dolefully considered his options. Realistically, he had two. He could fight on to what looked like sure defeat. Or he could retreat quickly and call the Americans to put pressure on the Indians.

Hmm. There was a third option too.

'What do we do, sir?' Hayat asked again.

Sharif got up. Screw it. Time to go for broke.

'Fire Nasr,' he said.

Far from the border, several miles inside Pakistani territory, an army truck ground to a halt and the missile launcher mounted on it slowly pivoted skywards. The launcher kicked and, with a shuddering boom, a Nasr missile blasted through a cloud of fire and smoke, and screamed into the blue sky.

Seconds later, when it had traversed a third of the distance, a tiny element inside the missile's guidance system twitched. Another second later, the Pakistani-made component which was actually a Chinese-made component which was actually a badly reverse-engineered US-made component, sparked and conked. The missile's guidance system went awry and the rocket began to stray from its flight path . . .

Miles away from the din and smoke of battle, Dawood Ibrahim sat slouching in a corner of his cave, bored out of his wits. His initial enthusiasm had worn off. His earlier relief at having moved to relative safety had subsided. Now, he was going nuts with boredom.

There was absolutely nothing to do. He could only spend so much time sleeping, eating and shitting. There was no other way to pass time. His mobile phone did not receive a signal. His neighbours, the Taliban jihadis, treated him with contempt and refused to talk to him. His attendant, although friendly, barely understood Urdu. There was no company except for the damn goat tethered to a corner.

He glared at the animal as it dully chewed a stack of hay. Inexplicably, against his will, his eyes travelled down to its rump.

Hmm . . .

Licking his lips, he pushed himself off the floor and slowly approached the goat, when a flash in the corner of his eye caught his attention. Reluctantly, he turned to his left and peered through the entrance. A bright dot had appeared high in the sky. Frowning, he stepped out to get a better view.

'What's that . . .' he muttered, squinting at the blob of light that was now rapidly growing bigger.

Realization hit him like a jackhammer. His jaw dropped and his eyes popped out of their sockets.

'OH SHIT!' was the last thing Dawood Ibrahim said before the Nasr nuclear missile slammed into the mountain and turned everything within a 10-kilometre radius to fine dust.

Battered and bruised, the three men wriggled out of the upturned car and crawled away from the wreckage, barely making it to safety before the vehicle exploded, sending burning pieces of debris flying in all directions.

Blood dripped from a deep gash on Modi's inner forearm. A bloody knee poked through Swamy's dhoti. Numerous cuts and bruises criss-crossed Shah's face.

That was the least of their problems, though.

The helicopter landed on the bridge 50 feet ahead, blocking any chances of escape. Qaal-za and an armed Saal-fa jumped out and strode over to them.

'It ends here,' declared the alien commander.

Alien captain Saal-fa cocked his gun and trained it on the three men on the bridge.

Staring into the barrel, a flood of thoughts rushed through their minds. Shah said a silent prayer for his wife and son, sad that he would not see them again. Swamy thought of his wife and daughter, and lamented that he wouldn't be around when TDK went to jail. Modi thought of the sava sau crore people of India and bemoaned that there were still a few countries in the world he hadn't visited and never would.

'Shoot them.'

The three men flinched.

But Saal-fa did not fire.

Instead, he leaned against the bridge's railing and casually crossed one foot in front of the other at the ankle. With his free hand, he pulled out a cigar, ignited it with a burning piece of wreckage from the car and drew a long puff. Then, in an utterly unhurried motion, he swivelled his arm to point the gun at Qaal-za.

'What the hell are you doing, Saal-fa?' croaked Qaal-za.

Saal-fa released a perfect ring of cigar smoke and as it floated gently towards the incredulous alien commander, he reached behind his neck and peeled his face off.

Qaal-za gasped.

'So this is what you have been doing all this while,' said Modi.

'How . . . when . . .' sputtered Qaal-za.

Ajit Doval chuckled.

'Remember when you guys went on a TV interview spree drumming up support for your demand?'

'Yes, I went to NDTV, India Today and a couple of other channels. Saal-fa went on *Newshour* and fainted midway through the debate. He spent the night at the hospital recovering from . . .' Qaal-za trailed off, his eyes widening in sudden realization.

'Well, that's the thing. He never recovered. The damage to his brain was irreparable and he passed away in the wee hours of the night. I decided to take his place and observe from close quarters what you guys were up to.'

The alien commander's mouth opened and closed like a goldfish in its dying moments, but no sound would come out.

Swamy stepped forward.

'Time's up, ET,' he said and shoved the shell-shocked Qaal-za to the ground. Grabbing his ankle, he dragged him to the edge of the bridge and held him dangling over the black waters of the Yamuna down below.

'Wait, wait!' the alien commander cried. 'I accept! I accept that my ancestors were Hindus! You said if I confess my crimes and accept my Hindu ancestry, you will spare me!'

Swamy grinned at Shah. 'That was a *jumla*,' he said. Shah grinned back, nodding his appreciation.

Swamy lowered his arm, preparing to let go.

'Mercy! Mercy!' cried Qaal-za desperately.

Swamy paused. 'Hmm. Well, the Constitution does provide for it,' he mused.

He put two fingers in his mouth and let out a piercing whistle.

Through the swirling fog down the bridge, sporting a dark bandhgala suit and black sunglasses, emerged the constitutional head of the Union Government of India, walking with the super-awesome gait of a superstar in a south Indian movie's intro scene.

'President Mukherjee,' said Swamy, 'I hereby file a mercy petition seeking clemency for alien commander Qaal-za.'

The epitome of awesomeness, President Pranab Mukherjee cast an imperious look at the dangling alien commander.

And in that moment, Qaal-za knew that he was doomed.

'Rejected,' the President declared flatly.

Swamy released his hold. With an ear-splitting scream, the alien commander fell flailing from the bridge and plunged into the dark, fetid waters of the Yamuna. In mere seconds, the irrepressible Yamuna did what it does best these days and the alien decomposed and disintegrated into nothingness, bringing to a fitting end the first alien invasion in human history.

FIFTEEN

The Promised Prince

NATIONAL SECURITY ADVISOR Ajit Doval struck a wooden match and watched its head fizz and burn. When the flame began to dim, he slowly brought it to the cigar and held it against its end until it caught a full and even glow. He drew a long puff, rested his head against the sandstone wall and gazed at the hazy Delhi sky.

There wasn't much for him to do. The aliens were gone. The Pakistanis had been handled. The political situation was back to normal.

For now.

He felt a buzz in his jacket pocket. With enviable economy of motion, he slipped a hand into his suit and pulled out his phone. An icon at the top-right corner of the screen announced that he had a new email in one of his secondary accounts. He tapped it open:

Dear Mr Kerry,

I sincerely apologize for this inconvenience. Because of security issues, I had to change my phone number once again. You may now reach me at my new secure number +92 311-459834.

May I take this opportunity to point out that Pakistan has been steadfast in its commitment to fight terrorism in all forms. Only last week, we eliminated India's most wanted, Dawood Ibrahim, after we received information that he was hiding in our Khyber Pakhtunkhwa province. And what appreciation did we get for this from the Indians? An attack on our peace-loving forces!

In light of this, I very much look forward to discussing with you the details of the OCO aid to Pakistan. We need it more than ever now, in order to restore the power balance vis-à-vis India and bring stability to the region.

I know you must be trying to reach me. Once again, I apologize for the inconvenience.

Hoping to hear from you soon!

Warm regards,

General Raheel Sharif

Chief of Army Staff, Pakistan.

Doval chuckled. 'Idiot,' he said.

With a few deft swipes, he copied the phone number from the email, opened Aam Aadmi Party's 'Become a member' page, pasted it on the form and hit the 'submit' button.

He slipped the phone back into his jacket pocket, took a deep drag from his cigar and gazed into the distance.

Nigerians rock, Doval thought.

The unconscious form of Deve Gowda washed up on the beach in limbo. The former PM came to with a start, sputtering and coughing, as he flailed about in hip-deep sea water. A massive wave slammed into him, depositing him further up the beach, where he lay sprawled face-down on the wet sand, dazed and disoriented.

'Kejri . . .' he muttered.

When he could breathe normally again, Gowda wiped his face with his hand, opened his eyes and slowly took in his surroundings. To his left was the vast sea, nothing but unending miles of water stretching all the way up to the horizon.

Wait. There was something else out there. He blinked to clear the blurriness in his vision, then breathed in sharply. On a tiny island about 200 metres into the sea stood the Statue of Liberty. Only Lady Liberty was holding aloft a broom instead of a torch.

Still prone on the sand, he turned his head to the other side. A series of rocky cliffs rose to his right all along the beach. One of those cliffs looked different from the rest, yet very familiar. A bunch of faces seemed to have been carved into the face of the formation.

Is that . . . ?

Recognition hit him a moment later. That was Mount Rushmore, and the faces carved on to the cliffs were US Presidents George Washington, Thomas Jefferson, Abraham Lincoln and Theodore Roosevelt. Only, they were all wearing AAP hats.

To the right of Mount Rushmore, on another steep cliff, stood a building that looked unmistakably like the White House.

'What is this place?' wondered Gowda, when two pairs of legs in military boots appeared by his side and the butt of a rifle dug into his back.

Gowda looked up and gasped. Two men wearing military fatigues, AAP hats and intimidating expressions were staring down at him. They were Barack Obama and Xi Jinping.

'You are coming with us,' said Obama.

Ignoring Gowda's protests, they hauled him by his arms and dragged him up the cliff and into the White House. They kept walking, lugging the semi-conscious Gowda along, until they reached a dimly lit hall with an extremely long mahogany table at the centre. They dumped Gowda into a chair at the foot of the table and stepped back.

Only one other man sat at the table, on the iron throne at the far end. He sat with his back to Gowda, facing a theatre-size screen on the wall opposite him, watching what seemed like a Hollywood flick. As Gowda's eyes adjusted to the relative darkness, he realized that there were many others in the room. He began to make out shapes and figures standing silently in the shadows with bowed heads and folded hands. As their blurred features grew sharper and brighter, he gawked in astonishment at Vladimir Putin, Angela Merkel, Queen Elizabeth, Abe Shinzo and many other leaders of the world, all wearing AAP hats.

Obama cleared his throat, the sound echoing loudly in the silence.

'Uh, sir,' he said, 'we found him on the beach, asking for you.'

The iron throne at the far end of the table slowly and tortuously swivelled around. Gowda stared in disbelief at the withered old man squinting at him with rheumy eyes. But for the AAP hat and the muffler, Gowda wouldn't have recognized him.

'Kejri, is that you?' he asked incredulously.

Jinping walked up to the old man and placed a gun and a totem on the table in front of him.

'Sir, he was carrying these on him,' he said.

Kejriwal stared at the totem.

'I know what this is,' he said in a tremulous voice. 'I have seen one before, many, many years ago.'

He set the totem spinning and watched as it pirouetted endlessly.

'I have come for you, Kejri,' said Gowda in a hoarse whisper.

The wrinkled old man looked up.

'I have come to take you back . . .' said Gowda.

Kejriwal's clouded eyes cleared a little. Something somewhere deep in his memory tugged at him.

'. . . to the real world . . .' he murmured.

'. . . where we can be young men again . . .' said Gowda.

Kejriwal straightened in his chair. The wrinkles around his eyes reduced, the mist in his eyes cleared. That ancient memory that was stirring in his brain grew less and less fuzzy.

'Where I am the chief minister of Delhi . . .' he murmured.

Gowda nodded in excitement, '. . . and Narendra Modi is the prime minister . . .'

Kejriwal's face instantly darkened and the familiar scowl returned in a flash. Springing from his seat, he wagged a finger at Gowda and screamed, 'YOU AMBANI AGENT! DID MODI SEND YOU TO TRAP ME?'

Gowda's mouth dropped open.

'VOLUNTEERS, ARREST HIM!'

'But . . . but . . .' squawked Gowda as the men hauled him away, 'this isn't real! We are in a dream! Can't you see? The totem is still spinning!'

'That's because this is a corrupt totem that isn't toppling like it is supposed to,' shot back Kejriwal. 'Volunteers! File an FIR against this totem and throw it in jail!'

The men took Gowda and the totem away. Kejriwal slumped back in his chair. His eyes clouded over and, with a dreamy smile, he went back to being the most powerful man in the whole world.

Back in the real world, Prime Minister Modi watched Kejriwal dreaming with his mouth open in 7, RCR's master bedroom.

If ever there was a win-win situation when it came to Kejriwal and himself, this was it, he thought. Yes, his brain might get scrambled when he eventually wakes up after spending all that time in limbo, but considering AK49, that might be an improvement, he snorted.

With a satisfied grin, Modi tiptoed out of the room, shut the door carefully and bolted it for good measure. Still smiling, he turned around, and jumped in fright.

'Maa Jagadamba!' he gasped, drawing in a sharp breath. 'You gave me a heart attack, Manmohanji.'

Dr Singh sat unmoving in the shadows, staring straight ahead.

'Have you been here all this time?'

Dr Singh answered with a blink.

'Um, it's all over, Manmohanji. I think you can go home now.'

Dr Singh rose from the chair robotically.

'*Theek hai*,' he said.

Modi watched the former prime minister mechanically make his way out of the house.

'I think I will also leave, Modiji.'

Modi turned around. It was Principal Secretary Misra, standing with a bunch of files in his hand.

'Sure, Misraji. See you later.'

Misra hesitated.

'Er, Modiji . . .'

'What is it, Misraji?'

'Um, I hope you have forgiven my . . . behaviour last week when you came to my residence . . .'

'Oh, there's nothing to forgive,' said Modi with a dismissive wave. 'Contrary to what others say about me, I am not a vindictive guy, Misraji.'

Misra broke into a relieved smile.

'So are you joining me and Ajit bhai for darts tonight?' asked Modi.

'Er, I don't know, Modiji . . .'

'Don't worry. We won't make you throw darts at people!' laughed Modi.

'In that case, definitely,' smiled Misra. 'See you later, Modiji.'

Misra turned around and walked out, oblivious to the printout of a dartboard stuck to the back of his shirt.

Alone now, Modi sank into the chair in his home office, sighing softly as he felt its reassuring familiarity.

Things were gradually returning to normal. Once Qaal-za had fallen, the rest of the aliens were defeated quickly and the violence soon came to an end everywhere in the country. Except for Haryana, where the Jats, after finishing off the aliens, went on to vandalize a bunch of malls, schools and police stations in the name of reservation, before getting bored and returning to their homes.

The casualties were surprisingly low. Yes, thousands of people had been turned into zombies by the aliens and were plodding mindlessly on the streets. But thanks to a herbal drug developed by Baba Ramdev that added another Rs 1000 crore to Patanjali's top line, they were all revived.

Well, most of them.

'All in favour of the Goods and Services Tax bill, say aye!' the chairman of Rajya Sabha had exclaimed in a special session called by the government earlier in the day.

'AYE!' reverberated the reply.

'All opposed, say no!'

A hundred zombies representing the Congress party, the Left and several other regional parties sat quietly in their benches with empty expressions in their eyes.

'The ayes have it, the ayes have it,' declared the chairman and, finally, after several long years, the GST bill was passed.

The situation vis-à-vis India's neighbours had settled down as well. Sanctity of the LoC was restored, and fighting reduced to the occasional ceasefire violation by Pakistani rangers to provide cover-fire to infiltrators. Pakistan PM Nawaz Sharif filed a complaint with the United Nations over India's actions on the border and invited the UN Military

Observer Group in India and Pakistan to visit Sialkot and take a look at the evidence of Indian excesses. US Secretary of State John Kerry advised the two countries to work out their differences through dialogue.

On the LAC, Chinese soldiers made a half-hearted attempt to retrieve a fallen spacecraft near the border on the Indian side and take it to their defence research labs for reverse engineering, but the moment alert Indian soldiers sounded a warning, they scampered back to their posts after urinating randomly on a bunch of rocks and flashing middle fingers.

Perhaps the surest indicator that it was business as usual lay in the papers.

'Doubts mount over government's claims of an invasion by the aliens,' said the headline of a Praveen Swami article on the front page of the *Indian Express*.

'Why nationalism cannot cover up the lies about the extra judicial killings of the aliens,' said the headline of the cover story in *Outlook* magazine by Rana Ayyub.

'Was Modi dreaming while India was burning?' screamed the 72-point headline on the *Telegraph*'s front page, accompanied by a high-definition click of Modi and Shah sitting back with their eyes closed in 7, RCR's bedroom during their attempt at inception.

'The chilling familiarity of the alien pogrom,' said the headline of one of the many editorials in *The Hindu*.

'Five hot pics of the vanquished aliens!' said the headline on *Times of India*'s front page.

Convinced that all was well with his country, Modi folded the newspapers, stacked them back on his desk and sat back in satisfaction. He grinned, basking in the sure knowledge that somewhere in Greater Kailash, Sreenivasan

Jain or Nidhi Razdan or some other NDTV anchor would be toiling hard at producing the next Blow to Modi show. Elsewhere in the Lutyens Zone, Rajdeep Sardesai would be raiding his Old Monk stock, seeking inspiration for his next sanctimonious, slyly critical tweet. Somewhere else, in a gymkhana or the Press Club or some random bar, a group of journalists and academics would be putting their heads together to come up with the next campaign.

Before long, they would exhaust all possible angles on the alien invasion and move on to the next story that offered an opportunity to bash him. The aliens would soon be forgotten.

Which would be a good thing too.

For none of these things need have happened.

His thoughts went back to the day the alien commander first asked him to help find the alien prince. There was no real reason for Modi to turn the request down, no basis for such a hard stance. He could easily have given up the alien prince, Indian citizen or not.

He even knew where the prince was . . .

Modi stared at the inside of his left forearm. The gash had healed and the bruises were gone, revealing fresh skin underneath.

Fresh grey skin.

He reached into the bottom-most drawer of his desk, flicked open a secret compartment and pulled out a spray can. Holding it over his forearm, he pressed on the nozzle and sprayed its contents over the grey skin, steadily colouring it until the entire area was uniformly coated and he couldn't tell it apart from the rest of his arm. He curled and uncurled his fingers, observing the play of muscles on his forearm.

The first time he had met the aliens at the airport, their physical appearance had stunned him. Not because they looked so different from the humans, but because they looked so much like him when he wasn't in make-up.

The more he learnt about them, the more the similarities grew. A sneaking suspicion about his own origins began to gnaw at him. And when the alien commander finally told him about the prophecy and their missing two-armed prince, he decided to fly down to his ancestral home in Gujarat's Vadnagar to confront his ninety-five-year-old mother.

Heeraben Modi had stared at her son for a long time. Then, she had risen unsteadily to her feet and, with faltering steps, taken him down to the building's basement. He had watched in amazement as she groped at the exposed bricks on one of the walls, then firmly pushed one of them in. A section of the wall slowly slid aside, revealing a secret room he had never known about. Inside the room, coated with a thick layer of dust, sat a space shuttle that was unlike anything created by mankind.

'We found you in this,' his mother had said. 'It crashed into our field sixty-five years ago.'

Modi had been too shocked to reply. Heeraben had walked up to him and placed a loving hand on his head.

'You are not from this world, *dikra*.'

It made complete sense. It fit. After his mother's revelation, there was no doubt in Modi's mind that he was the prince the aliens were looking for. And there was also no doubt that if he revealed himself, the campaign that would follow to pack him off to Mor would be unprecedented in scale and intensity.

There was no way he would go. How could he? His people were here! The 125 crore mothers, fathers, brothers, sisters and children of India. He had sworn to rescue them from poverty, starvation, inequality, corruption and every other evil afflicting this country.

Just like the prophecy had predicted, he realized with a wry smile.

So he did what he did, with no one any wiser.

Curiously, his teammates, even the sharp-eyed Swamy, had missed a clue staring right at them. In his act as the old woman in the first-level dream, it was the red pendant that had convinced Qaal-za that she wasn't lying about the prince. How had Modi known about the pendant? Fortunately for him, no one had stopped to think about this.

And now the worst was over. He had weathered the storm.

In all likelihood, the alien endeavour to take him back to their planet had ended with Qaal-za. The aliens weren't likely to send another expedition. Even if they did, he would be long dead by then, taking his secret along with him.

Yes, there was a slim chance that someone would find out the truth about him. But the great thing about being Modi was that he had been called so many things in his political career that being called an alien was hardly going to raise any eyebrows. No doubt, the media would go to town about it. His political opponents would lambast him. Experts would come out to show their outrage on TV debates. Intellectuals would pontificate on op-eds. His fans would spring to his defence. Everyone would fight and troll each other on Twitter, and the next day . . . life would move on.

So, really, he wasn't worried about that.

What he was worried about now, what scared the bejesus out of him, was something far more serious. Something that could threaten everything he had strived for so far. Something that could potentially deal a death blow to his chances of getting re-elected in the 2019 general elections and winning a second term as India's prime minister.

The Gandhis were missing.

Epilogue

SONIA GANDHI ROLLED over in her bed, smiling sleepily as she woke from the best rest she had had in a long time. Eyes still closed, she stretched her arms luxuriously and let out an uninhibited yawn.

'Mamma! Jupiter!' came Rahul Gandhi's voice from somewhere nearby.

'Yes, I know, beta,' she replied automatically, 'we need Jupiter's escape velocity to uplift Dalits.'

Lazily, she rubbed her eyes open and the world slowly came into focus. For a moment she was completely disoriented as her mind tried to reconcile the unfamiliar surroundings with the memory of her bedroom at 10, Janpath. Then, in a sudden flash, the events of the past week came flooding back to her and she remembered that they were still in the alien ship.

Outside the small sleeping chamber, Rahul was pointing at something and jumping up and down.

With an inexplicable sense of foreboding, Sonia leapt from her bed and rushed out of the room. The porthole that Rahul was pointing at no longer held a view of an airstrip in Delhi's Indira Gandhi International Airport. Instead, she was greeted by the sight of a black sky littered with millions of twinkling stars and a weird-looking moon in the centre.

Wait a second, she thought, peering at the moon. That is no moon . . .

'Jupiter! Jupiter!' Rahul cried in excitement.

'HOLY RAVIOLI!' Sonia screamed, and fainted.

Soon thereafter, the alien ship warped through a wormhole and emerged in another part of the universe, trillions of light years away from the solar system.

By the time Sonia came to, the spaceship had already entered Planet Mor's atmosphere and was fast approaching the space station in Mor's capital city. Minutes later, the spaceship smoothly touched down in the landing bay and the engine whirred to a halt. The doors to the spacecraft automatically opened and the inclined plane rolled out to the ground.

Outside, 50 feet from the spaceship, a hundred aliens stood in a formation, waiting for the passengers to emerge. Utterly terrified at what awaited them, Sonia cowered in a corner of the spaceship, refusing to budge. Rahul, however, had no such inhibitions.

'Yippee!' he squealed and skipped down the inclined plane jauntily. When he spotted the aliens, he grinned his trademark grin and waved at them like he would wave at the hapless folks brought to attend his rallies back on earth.

'*Bhaiyya, namashkar!*' he said, beaming.

The alien at the vanguard of the formation hesitated. Then, he went down on one knee, placed two right hands on the ground and bowed. Immediately, every other alien behind him followed suit.

'Welcome home, my prince!' the alien said.

They gathered in the castle grounds. Hundreds of thousands of denizens, from the far corners of Mor, as word about the return of the promised prince spread like wildfire. Watching the teeming millions from a window high up in the castle, Sonia was overwhelmed.

'I have never seen such a massive crowd. Why are these people here?' she asked.

Tel-pa, the alien leader who had greeted them at the airport and had been with them ever since, smiled.

'They have come for Prince Rahul's coronation, and to hear him speak.'

'I see. How much did you pay these guys?'

Tel-pa looked confused. 'Uh, nothing. They come in love.'

Sonia Gandhi frowned as she processed this.

Up in the sky, the two suns of Mor converged in an eclipse, imbuing the world with an orange hue.

Tel-pa rose.

'It is time.'

Taking their hands, he led them out into the royal balcony overlooking the sprawling castle grounds that looked rather like the balcony in the Vatican where the Pope stands to greet the faithful. A massive roar reverberated through the sea of aliens the moment Rahul and Sonia stepped out into the sunlight.

Tel-pa stepped forward and spread his arms grandly.

'My dear people of Mor, long have we waited for this day,' he rumbled. 'Long have we awaited the return of the prince who would lift our civilization from the depths it has sunk to, and put the smile back on the face of every citizen of this great planet. That day, my friends, has come.'

An alien female appeared with a tray that held a glittering tiara. Gently, with delicate fingers, Tel-pa picked up the tiara and placed it atop Rahul Gandhi's royal head.

'I give you Rahul, the Emperor of the Morons!' he thundered.

The roar that followed was unlike anything Sonia had heard on earth. Mor's millions clapped, roared and cried in a massive outpouring of emotion that mirrored her own. Tears of happiness streamed down her face at the fulfilment of a lifelong ambition that she never thought she would witness in her lifetime, or anybody's for that matter. So what if Rahul turned out to be a leader of Morons instead of humans?

When the noise died down after what seemed like an age, Rahul Gandhi rolled up his sleeves, stepped forward and planted two hands on the balcony's railing. The crowd went completely silent and leaned forward in anticipation.

'Bhaiyya, this morning I got up at night, and realized something . . .' he said with a stern expression. 'Mor is a beehive! To make Mor a superpower we need to empower women, bring in the youth, file RTIs and change the system!'

Sonia winced.

For a few moments, while Tel-pa translated Rahul's utterances in the local tongue, she wondered if their party had ended before it even began.

Then, the noise rose like a tsunami, louder and more powerful than the first time, as the vast legion of aliens discovered a profundity in Rahul's thoughts that had escaped the entire human race, and went completely bonkers. And just like that, Sonia's doubts and insecurities melted away.

'We can do this,' said Sonia. 'You will make a great emperor.'

They relaxed in the palace hall, drained after the emotional scenes at the coronation. Alien servants flitted in and out of the room, carrying refreshments for the Gandhis. Tel-pa stood respectfully by the side with folded hands. The only other occupant of the room was a wooden-faced alien who sat silently on a chair in the corner, ignored by the rest.

'And you know what's the best part?' whispered Sonia, out of Tel-pa's earshot. 'Considering that the average lifespan of an alien here is around 200 years, you would actually be a youth icon here!'

'I don't know, mamma,' said Rahul uncertainly. 'What about language? What about culture? I can adapt. I have eaten dal chawal at a thousand farmer households, but wouldn't you have trouble adjusting to all that?'

Sonia scoffed. 'How much more difficult can Mor's language be than Hindi? As long as it is written in the roman script, I'll be able to comfortably read out speeches in the local tongue. No problem. All I need is a right-hand man, someone who can implement my orders, someone like Ahmed . . .'

Tel-pa coughed. 'That would be me, Soniaji.'

Sonia regarded Tel-pa. 'How good are your contacts in Mor's media?'

'Excellent. I know everyone there is to know. I can get anything printed!'

'See!' exulted Sonia, turning to Rahul. 'It will be just like home before Modi came on the national scene!'

'I'm not sure, mamma,' said Rahul, fiddling with his tiara, 'just the thought of all that responsibility gives me a headache.'

'How about this?' Sonia turned to Tel-pa. 'Let's appoint a prime minister. He can take up the responsibility of governing the realm. He will be accountable to the people, as well as us. Do you know anyone like that?'

'Hmm, let me think,' said Tel-pa, scratching his chin thoughtfully. 'There are several options. Nab-pra comes to mind; highly experienced and capable. Then there's Ddu-chi; extremely intelligent, decisive and ruthless. There are some younger leaders too. Roor-tha for instance; erudite, charismatic and a terrific communicator. Then there is . . .'

'What about him?' interrupted Sonia, pointing a thumb at the quiet alien sitting in the corner.

'Uh, he's Nnu-ma, a highly educated and a very intelligent fellow, but a bit timid, to be honest. I don't know if . . .'

But Sonia had already walked over to Nnu-ma.

'So, Nnu-ma,' she said to the wooden-faced alien, 'do you think you can work under the leadership of Rahul Gandhi?'

Nnu-ma sat completely still, betraying absolutely no sign that he had heard Sonia, other than a blink of his eyes.

'*Theek hai,*' he said.

Acknowledgements

I AM GRATEFUL to so many for making this book possible.

Cleisthenes, the Athenian noble from 510 BC, widely regarded as the father of democracy. If it wasn't for him, my head would probably be on a stake for poking fun at our leaders.

Lord Mountbatten, for getting the hell out of this country so that our beloved *neta*s could take over and do what they do best.

Mohammed Ali Jinnah, whose espousal of the two-nation theory gave this world its first satirical state, Pakistan.

Charles Antoni, the owner of the Greek restaurant at Cambridge University where Rajiv Gandhi reportedly first met Sonia Gandhi and instantly fell in love—a landmark event that eventually gave us Rahul Gandhi.

The incredible readers of *The UnReal Times* who have been putting up with such rubbish jokes for over five years.

Ashwin Kumar, friend and superstar columnist of *The UnReal Times*, for his inputs and honest feedback that have helped shape this book.

Kanishka Gupta, my agent and also the greatest chaser after Virat Kohli. I still get nightmares of receiving text messages from him saying 'Done???', 'Any updates??' or 'Finish fast!!'

Milee Ashwarya, my commissioning editor, whose patience with me has been nothing short of legendary.

Roshini Dadlani and Arpita Basu, whose edits have transformed this book from an amateur's scribbles to something people would actually pay money for.

Manjul, for the awesome cover illustration.

Anjali, my wife, whose love, encouragement and threats motivated me to complete this book.

And last but not the least, the shower head in my bathroom under which I got 90 per cent of the ideas in this book.

- Apoplectic
- feckless
- Dictators
-